W9-BVX-199

SAHARA
special

SAHARA
special

ESMÉ RAJI CODELL

HYPERION BOOKS FOR CHILDREN

NEW YORK

First Edition

1 3 5 7 9 10 8 6 4 2

Printed in the United States of America

The poem "Autobiographia Literaria" (pp. 111 and 174–5) is from *Collected Poems* by Frank O'Hara, copyright © 1971 by Maureen Granville-Smith, Administratrix of the Estate of Frank O'Hara. Used by permission of Alfred A. Knopf, a division of Random House.

Library of Congress Cataloging-in-Publication Data on file.

ISBN 0-7868-0793-8 (trade ed.)

Visit www.hyperionchildrensbooks.com

Love and thanks to Russell and Jim, ever patient and brilliant. A debt of gratitude to Julie Froman, Steven Malk, Sarah Packer, and Donna Bray, whose support and insight made this book happen.

To Beverly Cleary,
thanks

CONTENTS

SAHARA

special

1

Me and Darrell Sikes

Why did I write them? Love letters to nobody, nobody who loved me back. They made me feel foolish and better at the same time. I didn't know where to mail them, so I just saved the letters in my desk.

> Dear Daddy,
>   How are you, I miss you, I love you,
> I still love you, I'll always love you.

Sometimes I wrote, *When are you coming home?* Sometimes I wrote, *So you're never coming home, or are you coming home?* Sometimes I wrote, *You can come home now.* Sometimes I wrote, *Why didn't you take me with you?*

I didn't keep a very tidy desk.

One day the letters poured out over my lap,

my feet, my teacher's feet. I got some of the letters back, but most of them went to the counselor, Mr. Stinger. The worst part of being in his office was watching my mom read those letters. Her face looked gray, like my letters were bad news, death news. Was she thinking I loved her less because I missed my daddy more? I felt like I was floating on the ceiling, like smoke from something burning.

When I came down from the ceiling, I pouted. I wanted my letters back, all of them. I was so mad. Isn't there a law against reading other people's mail?

Mr. Stinger took out a stack of papers, a file full of the history of me. No, not *the* history. *A* history. A history that didn't include when me and my mom go to the bookstore. I can pick any book I want, even a book in hardcover. That's the way it's always been. We never have much money, but Mom doesn't blink when the numbers ring up. She hands over the big bills like she was buying milk or eggs, something we just can't do without. I love choosing books by the pile at the library, too, and listening to my mom read them to me, when she's not too tired from working. She has been my best teacher. But that's not in the history.

Mom looked at the file and her face went gray again, and again I felt gravity give out. Look at that, a pile of messy work, of unfinished work, a sloppy diary of me since Daddy left. Why didn't I write more carefully in third grade? Why didn't I finish that assignment in fourth grade? I watched as Mr. Stinger fed my letters back into the long file cabinet. The cabinet closed with a metal sound, a safe full of evidence against me. Waiting there for when they need to pull it out and call me dumb.

When we got out of the office, my mom talked in a low voice. "What do you want me to do, Sahara? Say I'm sorry that I couldn't keep him? Fine. I'm sorry. I *tried* my best. Can't a woman get a divorce without her kid going special ed on her?"

I wanted to say, *Don't be sorry, Mom, I couldn't keep Daddy either,* but I was wise now. I kept my mouth shut.

"You gonna let Daddy walk out with your

brain, too?" she grumbled. "Well, then, there's not going to be a vital organ left between us, is there! You just do your work, Sahara. They'll see they've made a mistake. You'll do it, won't you?"

I stared her in the eye, but I didn't answer her. I knew I was being fresh and bad, but I couldn't lie and say yes. Do it for what? Do it for who? They took what I gave them, they took what I didn't give them, they used it all the same way, to feed the file. I was through with giving them evidence. They wouldn't get anything more out of me.

Mom looked at me, furious. I thought she would slap me for the first time in my life. She didn't. She stomped away. I stood there, wishing she had slapped me. You're supposed to put an exclamation point at the end of strong feelings. A slap would have felt like that. But instead, her heels clicked out her punctuation, *dot dot dot. . . .*

I couldn't see where my sentence would end.

That file full of letters meant I met with a Special Needs teacher in the hallway to get something called Individualized Attention, and let me tell you, working in the hallway with a teacher is like being the street person of a school. People pass you by, and they act like they don't see you, but three steps away they've got a whole story in their heads about why you're out there instead of in the nice cozy classroom where you belong. Stupid? Unlucky? Unloved? If I could have put out a cup, I would have made some change. People from my class would hiss, "Hi, Sahara Special" as they passed to go to the washroom, and don't think they meant special like a princess or a movie star or something sparkly like that. I pretended like I didn't hear, but oh yes, I heard, and you don't just hear meanness with your ears. My cheeks heard it and turned red, my eyes heard it and stared at the wall, at my lap, at my shoes. My fingernails heard it, and hid away in my teeth. I heard it all through my clothes and skin and blood and all the way to my bones, where it rattled in the hollow of me.

The Special Needs teacher told me her name when I met her, but I forgot it right away. Seeing her day after day, I was too embarrassed to ask what it was. In my mind, I just called her Peaches. In the real world, I didn't call her anything at all. In the hallway Peaches played board games with me and talked in a whispery, cooing voice like I was a doll and we were having a pretend tea party. I ignored her as best I could to keep from throwing up on her. She would sometimes ask me if I had done my homework and I would pretend I didn't hear. She spoke about using time well, getting things done. "Don't you agree that would make life a lot easier?"

I'd nod; sure, I'll agree to that. In fact, I thought, if I were *really* the school street person, I could *drink* to that, toast to it using the white milk in a carton they give at lunch, only keeping it in a brown paper bag. *Herrrre'sssss to the people who usssse timmmme well and get thinnnngssssss donnnnne!*

I couldn't help but laugh.

"What's so funny?"

I'd just shrug. She probably wouldn't think it was funny. I'd never seen her laugh. She'd write something down. Probably: *Laughs for no reason. Finds organization funny.*

Peaches seemed very organized. I bet nothing fell out of her desk in her whole life.

Then she'd ask if there was anything I wanted to talk about, and when I would say no, she would smile sweetly and look unhappy at the same time.

Sometimes Darrell Sikes would sit with us in the hall. I think he has been Special Needs ever since dinosaurs roamed the earth, or at least since the Declaration of Independence was signed. He kicked a teacher in the shins when he was in first grade, and when he was in third grade he was finally tall enough to punch one in the nose. At least, that's what people *say*, but who knows what's true? Mom says not to judge a book by its cover. Even so, I couldn't help but think that if Darrell was a book, the cover would read *True Crime Stories*. Darrell never spoke one word to me, and wouldn't look at me, and I thought he was a real gentleman for it. I did the same for him.

Darrell had a different set of manners for Peaches. Darrell grunted at her as if anytime she asked him something she was disturbing him from a nap. If we were playing a board game, he would roll the dice and move his piece backward. If Peaches asked him a question, he would answer by asking, "Are you married?" and batting his eyes, looking very interested. Sometimes he would smash everything off the table with a clatter, and swear.

"I'm afraid I am going to have to call your mother," Peaches said calmly.

"Well, don't you be *afraid*! You just go ahead and call her!" Darrell hollered. "You think she care? If she care, why the hell would I be out here in the hall with *you*?"

I told my mom about this, and all about oh how *funny* Darrell is, and the next day she came to the school and we had another meeting with Mr. Stinger and Peaches. "I want her out of the program," she said, "or whatever it is you've got going on here. I'm not sending her to school to sit in the hall-way with some lunatic."

"He's not some lunatic," corrected Mr. Stinger. "He's a human being with special needs."

"Special needs!" my mom sputtered. "The only special need that boy has is for an old-fashioned crack across his behind! My daughter isn't spending part of her day with a teacher beater."

"It's just what people *say*, Mom." I pulled on her sleeve. "Don't judge a book—" She shook me off.

"Your daughter needs support during this time," Mr. Stinger reminded her, and Peaches nodded. I thought to myself, that teacher just wants someone to play Uno with.

"Maybe we should ask *Sahara* what she wants," Peaches suggested, with her usual sad-happy smile.

"Is this Christmas? Are you the Special Needs Santa Claus? Ask Sahara what she wants!" Mom twisted in her seat and made a noise between a cough and a laugh. "Look, I don't have time for this. I know she's capable of fifth-grade work. She reads at home. She reads plenty. I think she writes, too," she said accusingly. I didn't look at her. She whirled around in her chair and growled at me, "Sahara, tell them you like to write."

She was telling it true. I read at home, and write, too, but whatever I write, I make sure I'm by myself and then, when I'm done writing, I rip it out of my notebook. I hide it in a binder behind section 940 in the public library, where all the books about Somewhere Else are located. This very paper, for instance, will someday be an archaeological find. Someday, someone will reach behind section 940 and find the dusty works of me, Sahara Jones, Secret Writer, and that person's life will be made more exciting, just by reading my *Heart-Wrenching Life Story and Amazing Adventures*. Someday, people will be glad I kept track. Someday, people will see I am a writer. And because I am writing a true story of my life I have to talk about school, since I am still a kid and it is a very big part of my *Heart-Wrenching Life Story and Amazing Adventures*. I am sorry to report that school is heavy on the Heart-Wrenching but so far has been running low-to-empty on Amazing Adventures. But I still go, because maybe one day I will have an Amazing Adventure there. Also, both the law and my mother make me go, unless I am sick with chicken pox or getting a tooth pulled or going to a funeral. So school is a lesser evil. Usually.

"Yes, I like to write," I squeaked.

Mom bounced her purse on her lap and smiled as if to say, "So there."

Mr. Stinger looked at me sideways for a moment. "Yes. The letters."

No, *not just the letters*, I wanted to tell him. *Not just those stupid stupid stupid stupid stupid stupid letters that grew legs to follow me around.* "So, can I have those letters back now?" I tried to sound like honey with sugar on top.

"Well, we need something to show that you like to write, don't we, Sahara?" Mr. Stinger smiled. "We certainly don't have any schoolwork to make that point. And this is what I'm talking about. Where is the work, Mrs. Jones? *Where is the work?* She doesn't do it here."

"You're saying she doesn't do her work? So take care of your business! Fail her! Fail her like a normal kid. The failure will be between me and my daughter, then. You won't like it if her failure is between me and you."

"There are serious repercussions to retention. . . ."

"Blah blah blah!" My mother can be very rude.

So they promised to fail me. "Remember, you asked for it," they said to my mother. They made her sign a form. Then another. Then another.

The door closed, and we stood out in the hall. I knew they were talking about my mom behind the glass, saying mean things about her, about What Sort of Mother Would Deny Her Child Individualized Attention. But Mom was smiling and I was proud, really proud of my mom not being afraid of failure. I am. I'd sooner not try than fail. They may think I'm stupid, but I'm not. Knowing I'm not stupid is enough for me, I'm enough for me. When my mother smiled at me, I could see I was enough for her, too. At least, for that moment.

I walked back to my classroom, past the little table outside the door where Darrell was sitting in the public of the hallway waiting for Peaches to return, drawing on the side of his shoe with a black marker. He didn't look at me and I didn't look at him. But in my head, I said, Oh, *thank you, Darrell Sikes, for being wild and nasty and rude and getting me out of The Program and making me*

Normal Dumb, not Special Dumb. I owe you one,
Darrell Sikes.

But I could not imagine how I would ever pay
him back.

2

My True Ambition

I like when my mom listens to me in the kitchen, when she asks me about my day. She always asks if there's anyone new I'm hanging out with or if I'd like to bring anyone by the restaurant. She asks even though my best friend stays the same: my very own cousin, Rachel Wells.

Rachel is a year younger than I am. Rachel's voice is like pages turning, whispery and smooth, and there's time in between each thing she says. She looks at her feet when she speaks in her paper voice, and her cheekbones get pink like she's telling you about the time she forgot to wear her underwear even if she's just telling you what she had for dinner last night. Rachel moved away for a while with her mother, father, and little baby brother, Freddie. She came back with her mother and brother. My mom and her mom find a lot to talk about together. Rachel left the same time my father left. But Rachel came back.

That is reason number one she is my best friend.

Some of the girls at school thought Rachel was stuck-up, but I knew she wasn't. For real, shy girls usually aren't. They usually care more than anyone else about what other people think. It's like they're walking on ice, and the ice is made of other people's opinions. But there's something not-nice about shy people, too. Something kind of stingy in the way they make you talk first, and then their answers are just one word. That's why it took so long for Rachel to join us upper graders in double Dutch. Always holding back. I had to go over to the fence, special, to get her.

"Rachel, oh come on, take your turn, jump, jump!"

But she wouldn't, not for the longest time. Even now, she always lets other people jump first while she turns the ropes. So reason number two that she is my best friend is because I always have to look out for her.

And reason number three is the fact that she's the only one who knows my True Ambition.

But for now, nobody can see my True Ambition, so nobody believes it. I only believe it because I saw it, just once, just for a second. I saw it in a crystal ball. All right, it wasn't a crystal ball, it was a goldfish bowl turned upside down. It was the middle of summer, and Rachel and I needed something to do, so we tried telling fortunes at the kitchen table.

"What do you see?" I asked Rachel.

"Nothing," she shrugged.

I waited for her to ask me the question back, which is the polite thing to do. I got tired of waiting.

"Know what I see?"

"What?"

"Nothing," I said, just to be mean. But I did see something. I saw my own reflection, turned upside down. Something in me tilted, and I knew. "No, wait, I see something," I announced to Rachel. "I'm going to be a writer." The words came out all by themselves.

"*You?*" She blew some air through her nose and shook her head.

"What?"

"Like, a *writer* writer? With a *book*? In the *library* or something?"

It sounded so good! "Uh-huh."

"What are you going to write about?"

"Oh, just . . . stuff."

"What stuff?"

What stuff? "Everyday stuff. Interesting stuff."

She looked at me like I was homework. "Everyday stuff isn't interesting stuff," she pointed out. She took out a deck of cards from the kitchen drawer and began to shuffle them. "Writing a book's too hard."

"How would you know? You've never even tried."

"I never tried 'cause it's too hard. I wouldn't write a book unless somebody made me. I have no *in-ter-est*," she explained.

"Well, I'm going to make me," I announced. "I have interest. I am going to be the youngest writer ever to have a book in the library. You'll see."

Rachel looked at me hard, like she saw the sparkling of Lake Michigan in my eyes. I smiled at her, and hoped she saw good things, exciting things. She blinked, and frowned. No, she just saw my eyes, brown. Brown like brick, like the high-rises that block my view east, block my view of the lake, block my view of what's moving with hard-ness and stillness and curtains hung crooked. The buildings hunker there, like boxes in a closet, blocking the way to hidden birthday gifts or other surprises the grown-ups haven't told us about. But I know exciting things are there, hidden, just a matter of pushing past.

"Then you better get a good teacher this year, Sahara," Rachel warned, like I have anything to do with *that*. Why does she have to talk to me like she's grown?

"I need *support*, huh." I flashed her a look. Rachel must have decided there were no more fortunes to tell, because, back and forth, she dealt the deck for War. She turned over an ace of spades. "Jeez, Rachel. Don't you ever make any wishes?"

"Well . . . I would like to be able to see without glasses. And to not have to watch Freddie so much. And . . . I guess I wouldn't mind having a cousin who's a famous writer," she said, collecting my two of hearts.

I bring home a big pile of books to read every week. I usually stay inside, because we do not live in a good neighborhood. When my mom sends me to the corner store, she watches for me out the window the whole time, and I see Mrs. Rosen watching, too. She is so old and shrunken, her head is hardly higher than her window box, but there is her head, like one of the flowers. I don't like the men sitting in the cars and drinking on the street, or the low-riders that pass with the bass so loud on the radio that my fillings rattle. Rachel and I are allowed to skate up and down the block, but in the summer Rachel usually goes to Cordelia Carbuncle's house to play in their yard, and I am not invited. I tell myself it is because I am older. I tell myself I am glad. I don't even like Cordelia. Rachel has lost her glasses three times on purpose, because Cordelia told her there is not one single famous model who wears glasses. So when I went to the dentist I borrowed a copy of *Seventeen* from the waiting room and drew glasses on all the girls. It made Rachel laugh, but she still tries to copy Cordelia and does what she says. For instance, Cordelia's momma lets her wear makeup. Rachel complained so much that her momma let her wear lip gloss on Sundays. It did look kind of pretty, so I asked my mom if I could wear makeup on Sundays, too.

"The only reason a girl your age should wear makeup is if she's a rock star or a hooker, and the minute you start showing promise in either of those areas we'll hop on down to Target and stock you up with everything you need," she promised. "Don't you tell your auntie I said that, now. What she does with Rachel is her business. I just happen to think there is nothing more attractive than a sensible girl," she said.

"To who?"

"To *who*? To *God*," she said. "And when you go to God's house, it ain't got to be no fashion show. You just come as you are." She gave me a squeeze. I think if my mom had to name her best friend, I might top the list.

But Cordelia tops Rachel's list. Rachel and Cordelia like to sit out front when she comes to visit. When the teenage boys say hi to Cordelia, she says hi back. Rachel doesn't exactly say hi, but she acts busy with her baby brother on her lap or smiles that terrible well-I-don't-know-what-else-to-do smile that makes me cluck my tongue and want to pinch her.

"How come you don't say hi?" Cordelia asked me once.

"I don't know them."

"They're just being friendly."

"They've got no business being friendly."

"That's why you don't have any friends," said Cordelia in a perky way.

"I do too have friends."

"Yeah? Who?"

"Beezus. Beezus Quimby."

"That's a *peculiar* name," said Cordelia.

"So's *Carbuncle*," I said. "Maybe if you didn't make fun of people's names, *you'd* have more friends. Come on, Rachel, let's go upstairs."

On the stairwell, I talked low. "Don't talk to strange men, Rachel. We don't have daddies to beat them up if they come bother us."

Rachel nodded and asked me, "Who's Beezus?"

"I met her when you moved away," I said, "and then she moved when you came back to town."

Rachel does not like to read. She likes to watch TV. So does Freddie. He bounces in his playpen when the people on the talk shows start throwing punches. Sometimes I am in her apartment, but mostly I stay in mine, which mom says is fine as long as I lock the door if she's at work. I open all the windows and the breeze and music from the ice-cream man floats through and lifts the curtains. I lie on my bed with my feet up on the wall and read. I roller-skate around the apartment until Mr. Martinez knocks his broom on the ceiling. I write in my notebook and rip out the pages to take to the library. I make lunch of canned sweet corn and boiled hot dogs, which I pierce with a fork and hold over the gas burner to turn the skin black, just like a real campfire, just like my daddy taught me. My daddy was a great cook. He even did it for a while for a living. My daddy could do anything. He liked to try new things.

New things all the time.

3

At the Library

Mom tries to get the Saturday morning
shifts at the restaurant. The tips are good,
and I love it because she drops me off at
the library. I can stay until noon, and then she
runs and gets me and brings me back to
the restaurant, and I can have pancakes. The
library is so air-conditioned that I have to bring a
sweater, and when I go in I just have to say
"Ahhhh," it feels so cool. I sit near the librarians,
like sitting near the bus driver on the bus, it's just
safer. They smile and say hello, but they don't talk
to me, which doesn't feel as mean as it sounds. It
just feels calm and ordinary. I sit in a big brown
straight-back chair at a big brown table of smooth
wood. I like to sit there and write my life story or

read the Ramona books by Beverly Cleary. When I read those books, the rest of the world melts away and I am on Klikitat Street. Ramona has a dad, and sometimes the mom and dad have fights. But they never break up. Sometimes I read the books twice, but the endings never change. In a story, if you write a happy ending, it never has to change. It stays happily ever after.

Sometimes the books have pictures of the authors on the inside back covers. It's fun to see what they look like. Sometimes they look much older than I thought they would be, or are a different color than I imagined. Sometimes there isn't any picture of them at all, just a description of how they live in Massachusetts with two dogs or something. But real, live authors wrote every one of those books, so the shelves are like lines of quiet people, sitting up straight and polite, waiting to talk to me. Someday I'll have a book of my own. Someday my book will talk.

The library has regulars on Saturdays, mostly mothers with babies and toddlers, but there is one girl I notice who is close to my age. She usually wears pigtails, but her hair is so kinky that they look round and funny, like mouse ears. She has a nick, some kind of scar in the hair of her left eyebrow that makes her look serious even when she is smiling. She is skinny and always comes with her skinny brothers, all older than her, who swarm around her but don't seem to bother her as she picks out books. She mostly goes to the arts-and-crafts section, but sometimes she pokes around *my* section, with all the books about faraway places. I have to watch her then, because I am worried and excited that she might discover that my papers are hidden there, but she doesn't. She just pulls out the books and reads them cross-legged on the floor. She puts a pencil in the spot where she takes out a book so she can put it back in the same place. She's very organized.

Once I was watching her and she looked up at me, straight into my face. I almost died. But her eyes were steady.

"Hi," she said.

I waved, even though she was right in front of me.

"You look familiar," she said, and pulled her lip, trying to remember where she might have seen me before. *Probably sitting out in the hallway at school*, I thought. I felt my cheeks get warm, and I couldn't decide what to say or where to make my eyes go. She shrugged, and seemed to give up trying to figure it out. "You're here regular, huh?" she said.

"Yeah," I said.

"Me, too." She smiled. "My mother makes my brothers take me. She hopes they'll look at some books, but they never do. They just wait for me and drive the librarians crazy." She let out a little laugh, and I joined her. "I'm Paris," she said.

"The city?"

"No. The girl." She looked in the direction of her brothers, who seemed to give her some secret signal. "Well, see ya," she said all of a sudden, and jumped up to join them.

I couldn't stop thinking about Paris and imagining talking to her. *My name is Sahara. The girl, not the desert. Oh, do you like to read? So do I. What do you like to read? So do I. I like your hair. How do you get it*

*to do like that? Sure, I would love to come over. Let me
ask my mom. . . .*

"Who you talking to?" Mom calls from the
kitchen. I did not notice I had said anything out
loud.

"Nobody," I answer. I rehearse some more, but
I am careful to keep it inside my head. I imagine
bringing Paris to the restaurant where my mom
waitresses. I imagine sitting on the high stools at
the counter with her. *Look what a big pile of pancakes! Oh, Sahara!* I imagine my mom's face as she
heads back to the kitchen, after putting down
plates for me and my best friend. The thought of it
makes my insides bubble.

The next Saturday, though, Paris brought just
one brother and a girl, a Spanish-looking girl with
long black hair and glittery butterflies on her
shirt. They leaned over a cookbook together, at the
big table. *Let's make this. Let's make this.* I sat apart
from them, behind them. As they left, Paris
noticed me in my corner. "Oh, hi!" she said. "I was
looking for you! I didn't see you."

Really? "Hi," I said.

"Didn't you see *me*?" she asked.

The question took me by surprise. "No," I lied. She looked at me, holding her cookbooks against her chest, as if trying to decide something. I looked away from her and pretended to go back to reading. *Who cares about you?* I thought. *Go bake your brownies.*

But she didn't leave right away. She seemed to stand there staring at me for a long time. Her friend waited patiently in the doorway. What were they waiting for?

"Wellll . . . bye," she said finally.

She left. "Well, bye," I said.

I sat for a long time and counted the books in a pile in front of me. I counted them up and I counted them down. But just then I didn't feel like reading any.

4

New Things All the Time

"You nervous about school?" Mom asked the evening before school started. She was washing potatoes at the sink as I packed a peanut-butter sandwich at the table.

"No, it's going to be fine," I said, thinking of being in the same class with Rachel and no more Special Needs in the hallway.

"You do, huh. Well, I hope so." Mom gave me a poison eyeball. I guess she was not thinking about my being with Rachel and no more Special Needs in the hallway. I slowly folded the foil around my sandwich and slid it into my backpack.

"All those books you read," she went on, not even looking at me while she peeled potatoes in short, fierce strokes. She was smacking them with the peeler like she wished they were my bottom. "What a waste, Sahara, what a waste. Talk about a crying shame, Sahara, it's just a crying shame, you read all the time and what for? Repeating fifth grade! How can such a smart . . . ! Tsk! Huh! I just don't understand you." She turned around suddenly and faced me, her chin jutting out and moving back and forth, but no words came then. She turned back to the sink. *Peel. Peel. Peel.* Trying to find me somewhere under the skin, the daughter she could be proud of. I just ran my finger over the smooth finish of my folders. I'm getting better at keeping things tidy, I told myself.

"I'm going for a walk," I surprised myself by saying.

"Oh, no you're not," said Mom. "Where you think you're walking to?"

"It's still light out," I said. I walked out before she could say anything and ran down the stairs, even though I could hear her through the door, calling me.

I walked toward the corner store, but once I hit the corner, where was I supposed to go? I still turned it, because I knew my mother was watching me through the window, and I was mad at her.

But once I was out of her sight I didn't walk anymore. I just sat on somebody else's stoop and put my head on my knees and cried.

My mom was there in a minute. She walked me back, holding my shoulders.

She sighed. "Let's just take it a day at a time, okay, Sahara?"

But I'm too lonely, I wanted to tell her. *I can't do it.*

But the sun rose again, on the first day of fifth grade for a second time. It rose and said, You're going to have to do it.

As I was walking in, no teacher was there, and the door was open. I took a seat in the back of the room, like always. Rachel chose a seat in the row in front of me, to my left. She turned and smiled apologetically. I smiled back. No hard feelings; the back row's not for everybody. She motioned to the seat in front of the one I'd chosen, but I pretended to be busy organizing my folders. I couldn't explain to Rachel that the seat in front of me was reserved, hopefully for someone very tall and easy to hide behind.

I looked at my new classmates. I knew a few of the girls from double Dutch: there was Sakiah and Tanaeja, and I knew Kiarre by sight, she's so tall and tough. I knew a couple of the boys: big-mouthed Raphael, Ernie who comes to the library sometimes, and Darrell, held back like me, legs spread, frowning in the back-row corner. Was that handsome boy's name Dominique? There was Paris on the other side of the room, and the girl with the black hair, too, chatting away. Paris waved, and I waved back. They seemed nicer than my old class, maybe because Cordelia hadn't made it back in time from her family vacation to Disney World, maybe because it was the first day, and everyone was clean, everyone was on good behavior. I looked at Darrell. *Better* behavior. The class was smaller than most. I noticed that this was usually the case when Darrell was in the roll. *Maybe I'll have new friends*, I thought fleetingly, but my mind was not really on my classmates. There was someone left I needed to meet.

The vice-principal was standing there. "Are you our new teacher?" someone asked.

"No." He looked relieved. "The fifth-grade teacher moved on over the summer," he said.

"She quit!" a voice called out.

The vice-principal frowned, but he couldn't tell who said it, so he ignored it. "Yes, well! Your new teacher is on her way."

"Is she a teacher from another class?" someone asked. Our minds raced. The patient kindergarten teacher, wagging a puppet on each hand? The short-tempered seventh-grade teacher with hair growing from his ears, the one who likes to be called "Lieutenant"? I shivered.

"It's no one you know," the vice-principal explained. "She'll be transferring in from some-where else. Be seated. Someone will be with you shortly." He excused himself.

A teacher from Somewhere Else sounded good to me. Sometimes, I wish I were from Somewhere Else myself. I wish I were from the sort of place that inspires you to write long sentences about the shapes of clouds and the smell of things growing. But when you're from Chicago, it's hard to write sentences that sound like anything except coins going into the change machine on the public bus. *Clink. Clank. Clunk.*

Clunk.

"Teacher's coming!" hissed a boy who was standing guard at the door of the classroom. "I think this is her!" He slid into his chair.

"Is she ugly?" asked another boy.

"Shhh! She'll hear, fool," snarled a girl. "Momma says, 'You never get a second chance to make a first impression.'" She folded her hands and smiled at the ceiling.

I closed my eyes and tried to enjoy the feeling of the teacher not knowing me yet. I think I could do my work here. It's been a while. But what's the use? Even if this teacher I'm dealt is a queen of diamonds, I don't want to give them any more material for their file about me. Their precious file, so different from my own file of my summer, tucked behind books in the low shelf of the library. I try to put this file out of my head and sit up straight.

And that's when I notice it is so quiet we can hear her coming down the hall. We are not even blinking, frozen like statues in our first-impression poses.

What's in *her* file, I wonder? And then I can't help snickering a little, even though it breaks my pose.

Because if they kept files on grown-ups, it would be a different story, wouldn't it?

5

We Got Her

$\mathcal{I}$n she walked. Our new teacher!

I blinked, and blinked again. Her hair was copper like a lucky penny, but when the light hit it a certain way, it seemed almost green, a deep green, like she colored it with a dye made from tree leaves. It was held back with sparkling dragonfly barrettes, but there was no help for it. It was wild hair. She was pale, but I couldn't decide for sure if she was white or Asian or Puerto Rican, or maybe light-skinned black. When someone is wearing lipstick as purple as an eggplant, it's hard to tell. She wore lime eye shadow and heavy black liquid eyeliner, making her expression catlike. She wore a yellow dress that looked like it was made of tissue paper, kind of old-fashioned and grandmotherly, but hanging slightly over her shoulder. Her bra strap was showing. It was also purple. She looked less like a teacher and more like one of those burnt-out punk-rocker teenagers who hang out in front of the Dunkin' Donuts on Belmont, near the L stop. Only grown.

Her arms were full of flowers. She opened up her desk drawer and pulled out a scissors, and sat down, cutting each stem at an angle. Then she swiveled in her chair and pulled out a vase from a cabinet behind her, and arranged the flowers. We all watched, caught up in where she moved the daisies and sunflowers, tilting our head along with her, this way, then that way. "Ever been to a farmers' market?" she asked the air, her eyes still on the flowers. "The flowers there aren't like the ones at the grocery store, oh no, it's a whole different deal. Imagine, these beauties, for sale in the middle of a parking lot! I swear, you can get anything your heart desires in the city, I don't see why *anyone* ever settles for *less*." She swiveled again, and pulled out a watering can. "Please." She thrust it at a girl in the first row. We all jumped—it was the first time she seemed to notice that any of us were there, and we had all forgotten where we were, too.

The girl left the room to fill the can. In the meantime, the woman sized up the space on the wall behind her desk. Then she whipped out a hammer, and a nail went into the wall with a brisk *bang, bang, bang*. We jumped again. She hung a framed diploma on it. If I narrowed my eyes, I could see it said MRS. FRUMPER'S FABULOUS SCHOOL FOR TEACHERS in fancy handwriting. She straightened it carefully, put her hand over her heart and blew through her lips in a satisfied way. Then she pulled out a table lamp with a shade of thin red glass, shaped like a tulip. Six clear crystals hanging all around the base of the shade shimmered and sang like small bells when they moved against each other. She unhooked each crystal and polished it with a handkerchief she pulled out from whatever it was she was wearing under her clothes. She held each crystal up to the light in turn, and squinted. We all squinted.

A boy raised his hand.

The teacher glanced at the clock on the wall, five minutes until nine, then back at the boy.

"Do you have to go to the washroom?"

"No."

"Then put your hand down," she said, hard and quick, like the hammer banging. The boy obeyed.

She hung the last polished crystal, and turned the little lamp on and off, to test it. "Working lights are important things," she remarked, again, to the air. "A light that won't go on, well, that's just sad."

The girl returned with the watering can. The woman filled the vase and pushed it forward on her desk. She felt for her pearls and adjusted them, making sure the clasp was at the nape of her neck. Then she sat, her lips against her fist, and looked us over one by one, with the concern of a dentist peeking into a very wide and decaying mouth.

The bell rang.

The teacher sighed and got up, moving around to the front of her desk and leaning against it, her arms crossed. She looked like she might be smiling, but the smile was tucked away like a mint against her gum and cheek. "Well," she said. "Another year.

"My name is Madame Poitier, Miss PWAH-tee-YAY. It rhymes with *touché*, a French word that means, 'you got me.'" She smiled openly then, even though it was the first day of school. I had never seen a teacher do that before.

"Most children call me Miss Pointy," she continued. We giggled. "Some children just call me Madame."

"My damn what?" Darrell called out.

"Your damn teacher," Miss Pointy replied without blinking, "and this seems like a perfect moment to talk about rules. What do you think some good rules would be?"

Kids called out. No talking. No pushing. No chewing gum. No taking other people's stuff. No swearing. No not doing homework. No pulling hair. No chair-kicking. No copying. No calling names.

Miss Pointy yawned. "How about, No rules that start with the word *no*? Haven't you kids ever heard the word *yes*?" She wrote on the board:

YES looking

YES listening

YES consideration

"What's consi . . . consid . . ."

"Consideration? Treating other people the way you want to be treated. If you don't like being pushed, or having your stuff taken, or having your hair pulled, don't do it, or you may be paid back in the same coin. That's common sense. YES common sense. And YES, hard work, harder than you've ever worked in your whole lives, so if you want extra credit, get a head start on sweating. I'm the meanest teacher in the west."

"Do you shoot from the hip?" snickered Raphael.

"You'll find out, cowboy." Miss Pointy's nostrils flared.

She wrote the schedule on the board.

Puzzling, 9:10 to 10:40
Time Travel and World Exploring or

Mad Science,
alternate days, 10:40 to 11:30
Read Aloud, after lunch
Read Together after Read Aloud,
Read Alone after Read Together
Art of Language, end of the day

What did it all mean? We looked at each other. None of us knew, none of us asked. We were all feeling too shy, except for Darrell, who maybe didn't care.

Miss Pointy passed out thick composition books with black-and-white marbled covers. "You each owe me two dollars," she announced as she passed them out.

"I don't got two dollars," complained a boy.

"You may not *have* two dollars now, but some-day you will. Then you'll pay me."

She continued to pass out the books, and one skidded across my desk. I stopped it with my hand, and smiled. It was nice to get something new.

"This is your journal," she explained. "You will

write in it every day. Begin each entry with the date. 'Dear Diary' or 'Dear Journal' is *optional*, or up to you. I'll read and sometimes comment on what you write, unless you make a 'P' with a circle and a line through it on the top of the page, like this." She drew on the board.

"This means, 'None of your business, Miss Pointy.' What you write is between you and the paper, and sometimes me," she promised.

"And the Special Needs teacher," Darrell grumbled.

"I don't like bureaucrats," she told Darrell, "but I don't mind cynics."

"What's a bureaucrat?" Darrell asked suspiciously.

"A tattletale who likes to write things down," Miss Pointy explained.

"Oh, like Sakiah," a girl called out.

"I don't know that Sakiah tells on people yet," said Miss Pointy. "So far, I only know that about *you*." The girl turned red; Miss Pointy winked, forgiving.

"She does shoot from the hip!" Raphael howled. We laughed some more.

"What's a cynic?" asked Paris.

"Someone who sees the world through mud-colored glasses. Mud's easy enough to clean up, though. 'God made dirt and dirt don't hurt,' that's what my little brother used to say. Right before he ate dirt."

We looked at Miss Pointy and couldn't help smiling. A teacher who had a brother who ate dirt! A teacher who would lend you two dollars! A teacher who was going to show us how to travel through time and to solve puzzles! So, she used big words and shot from the hip. Those two things could be overcome. All other signs pointed to human.

"Now. Line up against the wall. I'm picking your seats. No whining. Come on, come on. Now. You—there. You—there. You—there; no—there." I was relieved when I was seated in the back of the room again. When all of us were seated, she scrutinized the arrangement. "You," she pointed.

"Who, me?"

"Change places with her."

Second row. Rachel and I passed each other. How did Miss Pointy know I was . . . well . . . hiding? "And you," she pointed to Darrell Sikes. "Up here, too."

"Why I gotta sit in the front row!"

"All the better to see you, my dear," said Miss Pointy.

"Dang!" Darrell got up as slowly as if he weighed eight hundred pounds and sauntered forward. He finally slammed his book bag and body into place with such force, he could have been crash-landing off the top of a skyscraper.

"Oh, a thespian." Miss Pointy sniffed. "Your stage business is sluggish. We'll have to work on your pacing."

"What's a thespian?" asked Tanaeja.

"An actor."

"I ain't no actor!" Darrell exploded. "I'm Darrell Sikes, and you better watch your back, teacher!" All of us straightened. One boy made a sound, and was quickly hushed by another. Miss Pointy raised an eyebrow and scratched it.

"How is it I'm supposed to watch my back? I haven't any eyes in my back." She seemed genuinely perplexed by the request. She even glanced over her shoulder, to see how it felt. "No, I'd never be able to watch my back and teach at the same time. Never." She shook her head sadly, and sighed. "Oh, well. Can't be helped. Note to self." She wrote on a pad on her desk. "Assign. Back. Watching. Monitor. Darrell? Darrell Sikes, isn't it? Would you mind watching my back for me, since you were initially kind enough to show concern in that regard? It would be the first assigned job of the school year."

He was confused. We were all confused. But we were smiling. Darrell was not.

"YES make life easy on yourself," Miss Pointy said. "Don't mess with your teacher. Speaking of making life easy and of messes, I need your help to lighten the daily load. First, may I have a volunteer to stay and help me after school, clean up the erasers and such? Someone from the neighborhood, no one who needs to catch the school bus, sorry. This is a permanent job. I'll call and get permission from your parents. Your name?"

"Rachel."

There went my walk home. Oh, well. I thought of raising my hand as she named other classroom jobs, ones that would rotate so we all would get a turn: messenger, homework returner, current-events reporter, on and on. Maybe she could use more help after school, maybe I could ask her and she would say yes and I could clean erasers with Rachel. But I hadn't raised my hand in *years*. I wasn't sure my hand still knew how to raise. I lifted my wrist limply. It wasn't going to happen.

"You'll be leaving before lunch today. Just enough time to pass out textbooks." Miss Pointy let out a little private laugh. "Any of you ever read a textbook under the blankets, with a flashlight?"

We looked at each other, then shook our heads.

"Anyone ever recommend a textbook to a friend? Did you ever say, 'This is so great! You've got to read this!'?"

No.

"Anyone cry at the end of a textbook?"

We laughed. No.

"Huh," said Miss Pointy. "Well, they make lovely paperweights anyway, don't you think? I'll find something else for us to read for the most part. Now, while I'm passing these out, as I'm mandated—"

"What's 'mandated'?"

"Bossed. You work in your new journals. Some days you will write about your life—"

"Bo-ring," someone called out.

Miss Pointy stopped cold. "Who said that?" Nobody answered. "*Boring* is a swear word in this class. I don't want to hear *boring*. Ever." She picked up a textbook, a heavy one, and slammed it on her desk. We all jumped. "If that word comes out of your mouth you will be sent down to the nurse. She'll give you a shot on your south side to cure your boringitis and send you home. You just test me once and see if I'm kidding. Understand? Anyone here *not* understand?" Her voice was low. She really looked angry. She was crazy. She walked a full circle around her desk and took a deep breath. "As I was *saying*, you will write about your life. If your life happens to be b-o-r-i-n-g," she spelled, "then you had better learn to make life a little more interesting, because I don't read anything b-o-r-i-n-g."

"Why not?" Raphael ventured.

"Because. It's . . . it's . . . b-o-r-i-n-g." The mood seemed to lift as suddenly as it had come. "Now. I've told you all about myself, haven't I? How my first husband was a pirate, and I'm using this job to supplement my night job selling encyclopedias, yadda-yadda-yadda? Now, I need you to tell me everything I need to know about *you*."

Everyone stared at her.

"Make hay while the sun shines! Today! Go!"

We all started writing, or asked to borrow something to write with. Miss Pointy rolled her eyes, passed out a School Supply List and a *Lista de Utencilios Escolares*. Soon everyone was either writing or chewing on their pens and looking like they were trying to see their eyebrows. Everyone except me. I stared at everyone in turn, imagining what they would write.

Rachel:

I really don't see why I should sit in the back row plus something you should know is I need new glasses only my mother has not taken me yet so I don't see why I must sit in the back row where I can hardly see so please teacher please please change my seat.
Love your loving helper Rachel.

Or Darrell:

Somethin you shid no about me is I ant gon wach your back you wach your own back teecher p.s. you are stopid and ugly. and BORING BORING BORING BORING BORING BORING BORING

And then everyone else:

I like recess.

My big sister is going to have a baby in three months.

I want a Game Cube for my birthday.

I WANT A PET BUT IN MY BUILDING IT'S NO DOGS ALLOWED, NOT EVEN CATS.

Taco day is best in the lunchroom, but they don't give enough cheese.

I spend summers with my grandma in Alabama.

I like boys even though they can be sooo immature.

I have to go to the bathroom a lot, please don't yell at me.

soree techer, no speck inglish.

Then, I tried to think of what I wanted to say. I thought of saying how I was held back, but then I realized this wasn't something I wanted to say. I wanted to say I was sorry I made my mother feel

so disappointed, but then I realized that was something I should say to my mother, not my teacher . . .
and this, too, wasn't something I wanted to say. I
wanted to tell Miss Pointy I am good at looking at
things and smelling things and seeing things and
touching things and hearing things and thinking
things and remembering things, but so what?
These aren't things that are important to know at
school, are they? They don't fill in any blank, do
they? So all these things I know are a secret, I keep
them inside myself, in a box made of myself. Only
I seem to have lost the key and now I don't know
how to take it all out when I need it.

I wanted to tell the teacher that the world
looks different from the second row, that I liked
the flowers and the red lamp, and that I wished
she knew I wanted to be a helper even though I
didn't raise my hand. I wished she were a goldfish
bowl turned upside down and could see me
reflected in her, the way I want to be seen, without
my having to tell her. I want to be seen in a way
that takes her by surprise, upside down and backward from what's before her eyes.

The bell rang. A blank page stared up at me.

"Pass up your journals," she instructed. Kids started twisting around in their seats, collecting books from behind them. I felt panicked. I picked up my pen. I wrote:

I am a writer

And then my journal was one in a pile, being pushed forward. I could not tell which one was mine. I grew red and hot and foolish-feeling at the thought of Miss Pointy looking at those words. What was I thinking?

After all, in the end, she was going to be a teacher about it.

I am a writer

I believe you.

6

The Lion's Lesson

Miss Pointy is . . . pointy. Her nose is pointy. Her ears are pointy. Her shoes are pointy. And boy, are her fingers ever pointy. Sometimes even her voice is pointy. Especially when she says *you*. The *you* she's usually talking to is Darrell Sikes. Darrell Sikes always has fire in his eyes. Anything Miss Pointy tells him, he looks at her like she just told him she ran over his dog. He makes these grunting sounds and talks under his breath, until Miss Pointy can't ignore it anymore. She takes him out in the hall, she thinks we can't hear, but we're real quiet then, so we can. She says things like, "I can't make you do anything, it's your choice, please help me," when she's not too frustrated, but when she's mad, she says things like,

"Keep talking to yourself all day in that crazy way, you're going to end up a crazy man sitting at the back of the public bus with dead pigeons in a Hefty bag! How's that sound?" I hear Darrell saying nothing, and I feel mixed up. I know that angry feeling of grown-ups trying to push their way into the room of your mind, and I know that feeling of trying to hold the door shut against them with quiet and looking down. But I knew why I was angry, at my teachers, at my counselor. I don't know why Darrell is angry. At everybody.

Miss Pointy tries to get us to leave our problems at home. She stands at the doorway every morning, smiling like she's auditioning to be a movie star, but she blocks the door and nobody gets in until they use the trouble basket. We pretend to put our troubles into the big green basket she holds out before we enter. Our troubles are invisible to the eye, but they are heavy. She practically breaks her back, holding all those troubles for us, but she says we can't carry them into the classroom ourselves or we won't be able to work. She offers the troubles back to us at the end of the day, since they don't belong to her. Nobody's ever taken them back. Still, they seem to follow us and find us at home, like black cats.

In class, Miss Pointy ignores Darrell's Special Needs. She calls on him the same as everyone else. She waits a long time for him to answer. Then we all have to wait.

"Darrell? I'm waiting on you." Silence. "'I don't know' is an acceptable answer."

"How 'bout 'I don't care'?" he sneered. As a class, we made a low moan.

"Less acceptable," said Miss Pointy, and continued to wait. And wait. Finally, she moved on.

"Stupid Miss Potty," Darrell grumbled.

"Yes, Darrell? You have something to say, now that your turn is over?" Miss Pointy grumbled back.

"You called me a *barrel*!" yelled Darrell. Some boys snorted through their noses, because Darrell *is* kind of round and solid, barrel-shaped. He crossed his arms and pouted.

"I certainly didn't call you a barrel, Darrell. Why would I call you a barrel?" She sighed. "Please stop talking crazy talk."

"You always calling me crazy!" he roared.

"You're always acting crazy!" she roared back.

Then Darrell got up, kicked Miss Pointy's desk, and sat back down, his chest heaving. I would have been afraid. Miss Pointy looked unhappy, but not afraid. She got up and stood next to Darrell's desk.

"Excuse me," she said. She kicked his desk firmly with her toe. He jumped. "Huh. Did kicking a desk work for you? It's not working for me."

"You're not kicking it hard enough," said Darrell sweetly.

"Mmmm," she nodded. "I see. Would you mind getting up again?" Darrell stood. She shooed him a few paces away, and then she picked up the hem of her long ballroom skirt just slightly before punting the desk so mightily that it tipped over with a terrific crash and slid about three feet.

We stared.

"Ouch," said Miss Pointy.

She took her foot out of her high-heeled shoe and rubbed her toe. Then she hobbled back to her own desk. "It still doesn't work for me. Well, thanks anyway, Darrell. Or Barrel. Or Feral. Or whatever it is you want people to call you. Now let's get back to work."

Darrell-Barrel was too pigheaded to go and get his desk so he had to do his work on his lap. When we came back from lunch, the desk was set right again.

The point of this story is, don't try to out-crazy a crazy.

You see, even Miss Pointy's stories have points. She likes to tell stories about foxes and crows a lot. Crows putting pebbles in jugs and making the cool water rise. Foxes snapping sharp jaws at grapes just out of reach, walking away, not caring. Dogs losing bones to reflections in the stream. Ants working, grasshoppers playing. She told us a story about a fox and a stork. The fox invites the stork for dinner, but serves food in a flat saucer, so the stork can't eat. The stork invites the fox to dinner, and for revenge serves food in a narrow-necked jar, so the fox can't eat. "What's the lesson here?" she asked.

"Foxes and storks don't know how to eat dinner," said Leon.

"Fox should of just ate stork," Angelina observed.

"Maybe he was still full," suggested Michael.

"When people aren't nice, everyone ends up hungry and suffering," Ernie said.

"Hmmm, that's a good one." Miss Pointy rubbed her chin.

"No, it ain't!" argued Leon. "There's no people, just foxes and storks."

"When you go to someone else's house, sometimes they don't serve what you like," offered Mariah.

"Yeah! I slept over at Veronica's, and her momma served government cheese!" said Sakiah. Veronica turned around and sent Sakiah a stabbing look. "Well, she did!"

"Girl, your mouth is as big as a saucer!" Raphael laughed. "Come on, Miss Pointy. Tell us what's the lesson."

"Tit for tat," said Miss Pointy. This sent Raphael and some of the boys into such uncontrollable giggles, she sent them out of the room, one at a time, to the water fountain.

"That story nasty, Miss Pointy," said Dominique upon his return.

"I didn't make up these stories, you know. Aesop did."

"Why he always writing about animals?" demanded Kiarre. "Didn't he know no people?"

"He *was* writing about people. He gave the animals the qualities he saw in people: bitterness, perseverance, foolishness, trickery, pride. But Aesop had certain qualities, too, that made it so he had to tell stories for survival. He was a slave to King Xanthus, in ancient Greece. He was *mute*, he couldn't talk. He was ugly. They say he had a humped back, bowed legs, a potbelly, and he was short as a dwarf."

"Dang! That *is* ugly!" Tanaeja agreed.

"The Greek gods looked upon him and didn't just see what was on the outside. They saw he was decent on the inside. So they gave him the gifts of speech and storytelling. Do you think those were good gifts?"

"I'd rather be handsome," Larry admitted.

"Would you have known Aesop was ugly if I hadn't told you?"

No, we shook our heads. "He writes handsome stories," said Rashonda.

"I think so, too. He used his stories to advise the king. Sometimes he disagreed with the king's way of thinking, but he couldn't say so outright, or guess what?"

"They'd kill him!" We cheered.

"Off with his head!" Sakiah shouted.

"You gotta watch The Man," warned Dominique.

Miss Pointy did not argue. "Instead of disagreeing with the king, he used his stories to offer the bit of common sense the king might have been missing. Maybe he used animals so the story wouldn't seem too personal."

"He tricked him!" Ernie said.

"*Persuaded.*" Miss Pointy winked.

Then she told us a fable she said was one of her favorites, about a lion trapped in a net, who is chewed out to freedom by a little mouse. She asked what the story showed.

"Be careful of traps, whether you're a mouse or a lion," said Ernie.

"That's a good piece of advice for a king," said Miss Pointy, nodding.

"Or if you're a mouse or a lion," added Ernie emphatically.

"You gotta watch The Man," suggested Dominique.

"Perhaps," Miss Pointy said, "but please try to think of a new lesson, Dominique. That was not the moral of all of Aesop's fables."

Dominique slumped down in his seat, blushing. "I'm just *saying*," he muttered. "Ya'll better *watch* him."

"That's your daddy's moral, not Aesop's," laughed Tanaeja.

"You be quiet about my daddy!" Dominique said.

"Now, now, stay on business. What's the lesson of the story?"

"Pay back favors," said Ameer.

"Good," said Miss Pointy, smiling. "Anyone else?"

"It doesn't matter if someone is different, they can be your friend and help you when you need it most," said Paris. She was smart. Miss Pointy took out her Happy Box, a little box full of stickers she takes out sometimes if you impress her. We moaned, jealous.

"Paris is right. No one is so weak that on occasion he can't be a help to you. That's what Aesop meant, so that Xanthus shouldn't overlook the smaller countries in efforts to make alliances," explained Miss Pointy.

"What's 'alliances'?"

"Friendships. If there's a *conflict*, a war, you need all the friends you can get."

"If you're in a war, we'll be your allies," Ernie spoke for all of us. Almost all of us. Darrell had been quiet, burning his look into Miss Pointy's forehead all along, silently crushing his teeth against each other inside his mouth. I could see his jaw moving.

"I'll be counting on it," said Miss Pointy. "Let's write in our journals now."

I imagined what Darrell would write. Later I

was able to see, because it was my turn to check in homework on the chart. I stayed after with Rachel and peeked when Miss Pointy took the rest of the class out.

"I don't think you should look in people's journals," said Rachel.

"Just one person's, I promise," I said.

"Whose?""

"Darrell's."

She laughed. "You're crazy. He probably can't even write."

"Come on. Want to see?"

She leaned over, but then pulled back. "No," she said. "Curiosity killed the cat."

What a way to die, I thought. "Did Aesop say that?"

"No, your momma did. Get in trouble by yourself, cuz. I'd like to get out of the fifth grade." She went back to cleaning the board in wide, wet lines with a sponge. I read.

She a bich a big one why she go sayin
that I ant never sed nothin to her ima
tell my moma then will see

Well, I wasn't too far off.

"What'd it say?" she asked.

I thought curiosity killed the cat? "You were right," I said. "It's nothing."

7

George Gets Busted

After lunch we push the desks to the sides of the room and gather in the middle. Then, there in the soft rosy glow of her lamp, Miss Pointy shares stories with us. Miss Pointy says some stories are for reading and some stories are for telling. She told us the story about George Washington. He cut down a cherry tree, and then his momma came and said, "Boy, did *you* do this?" And he said, "Yeah," which I thought was stupid, and so did everybody else.

"Was he holding the ax when his momma come?" Raphael asked.

"I don't know. Probably."

"Busted!"

"Dang! He should of put the ax down and said he didn't know nothing about it."

"She would have known he was lying," said Miss Pointy. "She was his mother."

"Yeah, but she couldn't *prove* it."

"She didn't have to prove it. She was his *mother*," she repeated. "Do you have to prove everything to your mother, or does she just know?" Miss Pointy was looking so exactly the other way of Darrell that I knew she was thinking about him. "George Washington went on to become the first president of the United States."

The class was silent.

"So?" came a voice.

"Excuse me?"

"I mean, so what?" shrugged Raphael. "I don't get it. He chopped down a tree, he was busted, and then he became president. I repeat," he said, smiling, "*so?*"

"For one thing, he wasn't *busted*," Miss Pointy explained. "He had the chance to tell the truth, and he did. People tell that story because it showed he was an honest man, and that's what the American people wanted: an honest man. I tell this story to you because I think that same quality of honesty will get you far in life. Honesty isn't even really the right word, I think it's more like *accountability*." She got up and wrote the word on the blackboard. We couldn't see it in the dim light, but we could hear the tapping of the chalk. "Accountability means, if you've got the guts to do something, at least have the guts to say you've done it."

"How come we don't have presidents like that no more?" asked Raphael.

"Maybe you'll have to bring it back in style," Miss Pointy said so matter-of-factly, we all turned to smile at Raphael at once, and then we laughed. It wasn't a making-fun-of laugh, it was a gentle, embarrassed laugh, like we all saw the secret part of him for a second, the part that showed him all grown up, not just a smart aleck, but a man with a job.

"I don't want to be president!" His face was turning red, like the idea was buzzing around his head like a fly and frustrating him. "Anyway, the story's not true."

"Maybe it's true, maybe it's not, it doesn't matter," said Miss Pointy.

"What do you mean, it doesn't matter?" Angelina forgot to raise her hand. "The whole story is about telling the truth. How can you say it doesn't matter whether the story is true or not?"

"True things don't always happen in the world, where you can see and touch them. True things also happen in the imagination." I stared at her as she said this amazing thing so easily, as though she were telling us the time. "If it happened that somebody was living a life that made him wish for an honest man, so he made up that story, then there's something true about that story, even if the events didn't really happen. Do you see?"

I wanted to see, because I wanted to be like Miss Pointy, a woman who loved stories even better than TV. So I thought about this. I watched as some of my classmates pretended to think about this, but really were watching other people think about this.

"So, if it's not a true story about a man being accountable, it's a true story about somebody *wishing* a man was accountable?" I said as I raised my hand. I had to speak slowly. My mind felt like it was trying to carry a shallow pie pan full of water, and if I wasn't careful, it would splash and spill. The class looked at me like they looked at Raphael, but they didn't laugh. What were they seeing in me?

Miss Pointy was looking at me, too, tenderly, like a mother who doesn't need her child to prove anything, but is just glad to know what that child is made of.

"We can turn on the lights now," is all she said. "Time to write in our journals."

True things don't always happen in the world, where you can see and touch them

True things also happen in the imagination

I raised my hand today in both places

I didn't get a chance to write more than that because the door opened and there was Darrell's momma. "I've got words for you." She pointed a crooked finger at Miss Pointy and stepped forward.

Miss Pointy asked, "Did you stop in the office for a pass?"

Darrell's momma said, "I'm not going to stop at any office, I'm going to speak to you right *now*."

"Surely you can see, I'm in the middle of teaching a roomful of children," she said, real calm. I wrote the word *surely* lightly on the cover of my folder, in pencil, to surely use sometime.

Darrell's momma eyed Miss Pointy up and down, wrinkling up her nose at her fluffy dress. "I don't care what you in the middle of," Darrell's momma said. "You called my son a jackass in front of the whole class."

We didn't dare to breathe.

"I don't know where you got that idea." Miss Pointy looked at Luz and her eyes pointed silently to the wall. Luz got up and pressed the button twice, to signal the office for an emergency. Luz can be such a goody-two-shoes. But this time I was glad.

"You calling my son a liar?"

"Class?" Miss Pointy looked at us as if she had just asked us a review question.

"She never called him a jackass, and I have perfect attendance, so I know." Sakiah's squeaky voice came from the back. "He's the one always calling out her name and not doing his work, just messing around."

Dominique stood up. He is bigger than Darrell, so he's not scared of him. "He called her Miss Potty, but that ain't her name. It's Miss PWAH-TEE-YAY, it rhymes with a French word that means 'gotcha.'"

"Actually, 'you got me,'" Miss Pointy corrected him. "Thank you, Dominique."

Darrell's momma looked around at us slowly, but none of us said anything more. Then Darrell's momma marched right over to Darrell's desk, which was only about four steps away, because Miss Pointy keeps him in the front row. Darrell's momma took the journal off of Darrell's desk and whacked him over his skull, yelling, "Maybe you *are* a jackass!"

Miss Pointy stepped up and snatched the journal out of Darrell's momma's hand quick as a ninja and whacked her once on the hands, real sharp.

Darrell's momma's mouth made a shape like she was trying to inhale a hard-boiled egg.

"We don't swear in my classroom. Hardly ever. And we don't hit. Much." Just then, the door opened, and there was the vice-principal.

"Is there a problem, ladies?"

"Children. Excuse us for a moment. Please, continue to write in your journals. Maybe write the moral of the story," Miss Pointy said hurriedly, as they stepped out into the hall.

The door closed. We were too scared to speak. Most of us.

"The moral is, mind your cherry tree, George Washington," Dominique growled at Darrell. "I'll kick your behind till you look like Aesop, lying and bringing your crazy momma in here like that."

"Dominique, be quiet," hissed Tanaeja. "Ain't nobody in here be talking 'bout nobody's momma."

"Anyway, that isn't the moral of the story," said Kiarre calmly, bigger than all of us and afraid of nothing. "The moral is just what Miss Pointy said. 'Stop in the office for a pass.'"

This satisfied us, and we didn't speak any more. Darrell didn't look up. He was writing in his journal, like Miss Pointy asked. I started thinking about him. How does it feel to have a momma who doesn't know anything about you? A momma who needs you to prove whether or not you're a liar, who doesn't just know?

One thing for sure, Darrell Sikes makes school more interesting.

I know it's nosy, but I couldn't wait until I had another chance to see his journal. I hoped it had a *sorry* in it.

She a bich why she hit me in front of the hole class I dint do NOTHIN and futhumore why dint miss POTTY POTTY POTTY say nothin bout callin me baril, she so foney. P.S. Domaneek better whach his tale Im gon whip him bad.

As I mentioned to your mother, we do not swear in class. You will write "bitch" ten times so you learn to spell it correctly and then I will never see it or hear it from you again. School language, please.

Miss Potty

(only you may call me that, then we'll call it even)

speekin of LANGWAGE Miss oo-la-la why don't you speek eenglish, this is the younited states of america not planit of the apes. You talk fancy but I no a secrit, you ant all that MISS POTTY

Darrell, see me during recess this week, I'm going to teach you the brand of English I speak. I'm inviting Dominique, so you won't be lonely. You don't have to thank me.

Miss Oo-la-la

(beats Miss Potty any day)

8

The Way Things Are Built

Miss Pointy loves to show us slides of the way things are built. She says it's *architecture*. The way Miss Pointy talks about architecture, it's as if it is a person, something built from the inside out. She gave us drinking straws to try to construct what we think the skeletons of skyscrapers look like. "Beams are the bones that hold the body," she said. While we worked, she showed us black-and-white photographs of men balancing on these beams, eating lunch, talking, at home in the sky. The sky is definitely Somewhere Else. Looking at these men, I thought about Heaven. I wondered if my father was working construction.

This arch in Paris, France. That dome in Florence, Italy. This wall, that pillar, this doorway, that window. Miss Pointy pointed out details in stone that looked like piped whipped cream. She showed us palaces, cliff dwellings, tipis, shanties, barns. Fountains, filigrees, spires, gargoyles watching from on high, stairs, pillars, bridges. I love these words, I couldn't write them down fast enough, magic words that bring your mind to Somewhere Else. But they aren't all somewhere else. Some of them are right here in Chicago. She showed us pictures of our own city. The Bahá'í Temple, Wrigley Field, the Water Tower, the Tribune building. She showed us the beautiful stones in the Graceland cemetery. She showed us the pink Edgewater Beach apartments off of Lake Shore Drive near Bryn Mawr, from the days when Uptown had movie studios and fine hotels. She showed us the skyline of Navy Pier, the long jetty with its elegant Ferris wheel slowly turning amid the seagulls. She said she would take us to see Buckingham Fountain at night when the weather gets warm, she said she'd treat us all to *churros* and we could watch the colors change in the water. She said we would all go to the bathroom at the Palmer House Hotel.

She said she would take us to the top of the Sears Tower someday. We were afraid, but we didn't mention it exactly.

"Grandma says skyscrapers is a sin, it's bad for man to try to reach God," Angelina said.

"I think it's a sin not to try," said Miss Pointy. "If we are all God's children, as your grandmother would probably say, then isn't it natural for a child to reach up to a parent?"

I knew the answer. But then I had another question: isn't it just as natural for a parent to reach for his child? When I thought of my father's architecture, I hung my head and closed my eyes. In my imagination I heard the roar of heavy machinery approaching, I felt the walls of myself shimmy and crack. Even though I told myself it was in my head, I had to hold on to my desk for a minute, a hand tight on each side, thinking the words I didn't write.

Dear Daddy, My heart is a shanty. So why did you send a wrecking ball? Why didn't you build me a house instead, or a skyscraper a million stories high?

The only stories I can build are on paper, but I thought of that hungry file cabinet in the counselor's office and I didn't dare write anything here at school. In my mind's eye, I wrote the letter to my father. In my mind's eye, I crumpled that letter into a ball.

Then the sound I imagined rolls away. I blinked, and I was surprised to see walls still standing all around me. Everyone but me was building skyscrapers.

"Finish your structures for homework," said Miss Pointy.

Everyone finishes their homework for Miss Pointy, because Miss Pointy gives beautiful glittery stickers for prizes. Luz gets a lot of stickers from Miss Pointy. I am not the sticker police, I just know this because I sit right behind her to the left. I couldn't help but notice how after a short time had passed, her collection had spread all over the front of her journal like measles. Then it was so full, she had to start putting them on the inside cover.

"Doesn't that make your journal kind of heavy?" I asked.

"Eees okay." Luz smiled at me. "I don mind."

Whenever a paper is passed back, I see Luz bounce just a little bit on her bottom, she's so excited. Then she takes her fingernail and goes pick-pick-pick at the corner of the sticker until it comes off of her paper, and she re-sticks it on her journal cover. Luz isn't all that smart, but she gets them anyway, because Miss Pointy says trying your best is a success in itself.

What does that make me? I don't have a single sticker.

Once Miss Pointy saw that Luz's cover was filled and she said, "When I was a little girl, I collected stickers, too," and they smiled at each other. I guess I wasn't the only one who overheard this gross conversation, because then all the girls and some of the boys started peeling stickers off their papers and sticking them on their journals. But I'll bet two bags of chips Miss Pointy brought her old collection from home and secretly gave it to Luz, because Luz suddenly turned up with glossy photo-album pages of stars and hearts and unicorns and what-all. I also think Miss Pointy secretly gave Ernie a book of Aesop's Fables, too. For keeps! I complained to Rachel about this.

"I don't want a book of Aesop's Fables." She shrugged.

"Even if she offered it to you?"

"She didn't offer it to me. She offered it to Ernie. I guess she must have been tired of him asking for the same old stories over and over." I must have been looking grumpy, because Rachel added, "I think it was nice of her. Don't be jealous."

"Jealous!" There was no use talking to Rachel. I suppose she also thought it was nice that Miss Pointy gave Boris the same book, even though he doesn't speak a word of English, not one word! Ernie can go over to Boris's desk and look at the book with him whenever he wants, he doesn't even have to ask, he just goes, and there they are, Miss Pointy doesn't even look up.

This class has class pets.

I wanted to write, *Why does some girl who just learned to speak English two years ago get twenty million stickers, while I get zero?* But then I remembered what Miss Pointy's answer would be. She even wrote it in my journal, in red ink, after I hadn't done a journal entry in four days straight.

A writer writes.

Why can't she be normal and say "Do your work" like any other teacher? Why can't she take me out in the hall like I was Darrell Sikes and tell me that I'm capable of so much more, talk about disappointment and calling my mother and grades? But no, she's trickier than that. *A writer writes,* she says. Like she's saying, *Are you writing, or are you nobody?* That's the way it feels.

Maybe she doesn't mean it like that, maybe she's just giving matter-of-fact writing advice, like

she always does in my journal. I understand some
of it, like

*If you hear a good word that
belongs to someone else, write it down
somewhere so it belongs to you, too.*

I already do that. What's she telling me that
for?

*Don't ever end a story, "And then
I woke up. It was just a dream!"
That's a very cheap trick.*

*Don't kill your characters. The
worst ones should go on and on and
on, just like in real life.*

Some of her comments I don't understand
very well.

*Kid vs. nature, kid vs. kid, kid
vs. himself. Pick a fight.*

*Words that don't mean much:
nice, pretty, ugly, bad, good.*

*Know how to tell who's the main
character? It's not always the one
you like the best. It's the one who
changes.*

During journal time, I stare at her words, moving each piece of advice in my mind like a hand
explores a stone in a collection of stones. But the
same one stands out every time: "A writer writes."
This is not a stone, this is a rock, and I don't want
it. I just want a sticker, and I know she'd give me a
thousand stickers if I would only do my work. But
I'm no begging dog. I can buy me all the stickers I
want at the store.

I taste the flavor of sour grapes, like the fox on
the cover of Ernie's book of fables. I swallow it
down.

Usually Miss Pointy hands back the journals,
but one bad day she was busy fixing some equip-

ment in the back of the room, so she let Leon pass the journals back. He wasn't paying attention and gave them to all the wrong people. A star-covered journal appeared on my desk. I quickly slid it under my desk and into my lap, and stared at the collection of bears and clowns and unicorns and brightly colored words:

GOOD JOB!

YOU CAN DO IT!

FAR OUT!

I'M IMPRESSED!

In the left corner was a star with a rainbow streaming behind it. All that glitters is not gold, says Aesop, but if it was gold glitter, that was good enough for me. I felt my finger tweaking at one of the star's points, only it wasn't my finger, it was a robot's finger, programmed to do some other, bad girl's bidding. I felt the useless resistance of the sticker, trying to stay on poor Luz's notebook. The star curled away.

Luz raised her hand, waved it, panicked. "Mees Pointee! Thees ees not my journal!"

"This isn't mine, either," said Ernie.

"Well, don't open them! They're private!" Everyone opened them. "Darrell! Sakiah! Hey! Close those books!" Miss Pointy directed, turning away from the VCR to confiscate the journals. "I'll pass them back myself. Heavens, Leon, can't I count on you?" I felt Luz's notebook being lifted from my grasp. I hadn't had a chance to put the star back. I meant to. I was just seeing how sticky it was. My journal was handed back to me. I stuck the star on the inside cover. I glanced over at Luz. She was looking at the cover of her journal, then she began to crane her neck. Would she raise her hand? No, she just leaned back hard in her chair, and slowly ran her fingers across the stickers she had left. Plenty of stickers, in my opinion. She didn't write anything, she just made fists and rested her cheeks on them. She frowned.

"Wanna see what I wrote in my journal?" Paris offered, tapping my shoulder from behind across the aisle. I was surprised.

"Sure," I said.

I read:

Miss Pointy, Please DO read.
IMPORTANT!!!

Luz's collection isn't the only sticky thing in this room. Someone has STICKY FINGERS. Just thought you should know.

Mom says, in the city, there's a million windows. Someone's always watching you, seeing what you are doing, what's happening to you. It always made me feel safe, like wherever I was, I had guardian angels. I realized, suddenly, that maybe other people have guardian angels, too. I handed the journal back to Paris, careful to keep my mouth a straight, closed line. Then I couldn't help it. I turned back to Paris and opened my mouth.

"What do you want?" I hissed.

"Not a thing." She smiled innocently. Paris plays with Luz on the playground every day. Luz's best friend, kitty-corner behind me! How could I have been so careless!

"I was going to give it back," I turned around again.

"So give it," Paris folded her hands.

"Stop acting so grown-up," I growled.

"Sahara? Is there a problem?" Miss Pointy asked from the back of the room. "Please stop turning around and get to work. You, too, Paris."

Paris's smile makes me think I am going to go crazy.

We were supposed to write about architecture where we live. I stared at my blank page. Finally I wrote,

Do teachers have secrets?

That's all I wrote. Certainly not enough to earn a sticker. Suddenly, I realized I couldn't hand this journal back up to Miss Pointy, not with the star on the inside cover. So I peeled it off. It ripped a little, and curled into a coil. What should I do with it? I wondered. I didn't know, so I dropped it on the floor. From the corner of my eye, I saw Paris dip down to get it. Time went slowly.

Finally, Miss Pointy started collecting the

journals. Paris half-stood, reaching over my desk. "Here, Luz!" she called.

Luz took it, but she did not look happy. "Eees dirty. There's dirt all over eet," she remarked. "Why you take eet, Paris?"

Paris looked shocked. "Me!"

"I thought we were friends," she said to Paris.

"I didn't take it," said Paris.

"Then who deed?" Luz raised her hand. Paris seemed frozen, searching for her breath. Finally, she glared at me, set back down and crossed her arms.

"Yes, Luz?" Miss Pointy turned. I braced myself.

"I need some escotch tape," said Luz. "One of my esteekers ees loose."

Miss Pointy frowned, and got some clear Con-Tact paper. She showed Luz how to cover her whole book with the film. "Now, none of them will come off," she explained. Luz looked up grate-fully. "I'm sorry I didn't think of it sooner."

Me, too, I thought.

At recess, Paris marched up to me.

"You gonna take care of your business or not?"

I couldn't even look at Paris in the eye.

"Cordelia told me you were bad, but I didn't believe her. I told her I like to make up my own mind. I thought we could be friends. Thanks, Sahara." She clucked her tongue, disgusted. I saw her feet turn and walk away.

I watched Paris and Luz make careful circles as they played, not crossing each other's paths. I leaned against the chain-link fence with Rachel, who said nothing, as usual. I had a conversation with myself, instead. More of a lecture. About how I read all those books, wishing life could be like what I read, wishing there would be such things as heroes and adventures. But a hero is the one who does what's hard, like Paris, taking the blame and losing a friend. Or Luz, saying words in another language, a language her own mother doesn't speak. Could I do what she does, take a risk with every word? The answer made my cheeks feel hot.

I looked at Kiarre, overgrown and pushy, trying so hard to be the policewoman instead of the criminal. Raphael, with his big mouth, wanting to laugh even if it's at himself. I thought about Ernie, hiding from the gangs in the library after school, and being called a chicken. Sakiah, telling on everyone and talking too much, tagging along like everybody's little sister. Even Darrell, beaten in front of the whole class, held back, mean and slow but present, every day; is school still better than home? He was a hero, too. *They told me you were bad, Darrell, but I didn't believe them. I like to make up my own mind. I thought we could be friends. . . .*

I looked at my classmates, sprawled across the playground, their noise swirling all around me. I *like my class*, I thought, surprised. Aside from Cordelia, the rest of them were decent, not one of them had yet mentioned how I was held back, not one of them called me stupid or slow. They could have, couldn't they? What do they see, us girls against the chain-link fence? Is Rachel a shy girl, or a snob? Am I a mysterious girl, a secret-keeper, or just a thief, a girl who steals other people's rewards, telling herself she could earn them herself if she really wanted? If she really wanted! I turned away, my back to everyone, and closed my eyes tight.

Rachel noticed. "Are you okay?" I shook my head violently. I thought of saying, *Let's play with everyone else. Let's not stand here, by ourselves.* But I couldn't, not today. I knew I was standing where I belonged.

Before we entered the classroom, I whispered to Miss Pointy, "I need the trouble basket." She motioned to me with her finger, and pulled it out from under her desk. She held it low, by her knees, so it was private. I pretended to put my troubles in it. I put and I put and I put, while she watched silently, holding the handle with both hands. Then I looked at her and nodded that I was through.

I went back to my seat. My stomach had started to hurt. I put my head down and hid in the dark of my own arms. Miss Pointy didn't call on me for the rest of the day.

9

Miss Pointy Gets Me
Where I Live

Rachel's brother, Freddie, was to blame for our stomach flu. Rachel and I were taking turns holding him, cuddling him, kissing him. He's so chubby, like a baby doll, we couldn't resist. Until he started throwing up. Then we handed him back to my aunt. Two days later, Rachel and I were throwing up, too.

We were lying with our feet sticking in each other's faces on the sofa in my living room. Rachel's momma couldn't take off any more work, so my mom took a sick day to take care of us. The hours passed slowly. The drone of cartoons had become wearisome, and the flickering of the screen began to nauseate us. Freddie drooled in his playpen, not knowing or caring what he had done to us with his evil, germy cuteness.

We tried entertaining ourselves by drawing pictures of each other. I stared at Rachel. Her hair looked like the Bride of Frankenstein. Her eyes had half-moons of green underneath, and the corners of her mouth had little fans of spittle. I didn't mention this. I imagined I looked the same. We showed each other our unimpressive work.

"Now what do you want to do?" I asked her.

"I don't know." Rachel shrugged.

We lay there, weak and staring at each other, thinking the word that Miss Pointy had trained us not to dare to say aloud. B-*o-r-i-n-g*.

"Let's eat toast," I suggested. We ate our toast, crust first, then middle.

"Ooogh," said Rachel.

"Mom!" I called.

Mom came running in. She put her arms around Rachel, and walked her to the bathroom. Strange, painful, wet cries drifted down the hallway. Pungent smells, and then the sound of teeth being brushed, the toilet being flushed, Lysol being sprayed. Rachel was walked back after a time, looking like Kiarre had given her the once-over.

"Oooogh," said Rachel.

"Now what do you want to do?" I asked.

"Sahara! Leave her be," Mom said, pulling over a pail within puke-shot. "Do you need one of these, too?"

"No, I don't think so," I said. "I feel okay. Except when I look at *her*."

Rachel smiled from the other end of the sofa, her eyes closed. Then she frowned, and leaned over the pail. She made some noises, but nothing came out.

"Don't excite her. Read a book. Read to her. Do something quietly."

"Her toes are about two million degrees," I complained. "I think I'm getting blisters where her toes are touching my leg."

My mother felt Rachel's head. "Oh, honey," she said, and got some Tylenol. Rachel swallowed the pills, and took noisy, experimental sips from a glass of water. Mom and I watched with interest. Nothing came up. "Try to sleep, boo-boo." Then she turned to me. "You let her sleep," she warned.

After Mom left the room, Rachel lay there

with a cool rag on her forehead, moaning exotically. "Let's pretend you're sick," I suggested.

"I am sick," she reminded me.

"No, really sick. We're sisters, lost in the desert."

"Nnnngghhh. Too hot."

"All right, the tundra. I'm nursing you back to health on seal blubber and fish."

Rachel leaned over the pail.

"Sahara!" My mother's voice scolded from the kitchen.

I whispered. "It seems like you're close to the end, but don't go on that ice drift, Rachel-Quiet-River-Flowing. Your betrothed, Darrell-Whose-Mother-Pounds, will be heartbroken." Rachel eyed me from over the pail.

"Make it Dominique," she croaked, leaning back into the pillows.

I waited for her to ask me who I liked. The question never came.

"I am your older sister. I have to get married first," I explained. "Who will it be?"

Rachel snored delicately at the other end of the sofa. Freddie shifted in the playpen, sucking on the paw of his worn-out teddy bear. I sighed, and picked up *Julie of the Wolves*. Time moved more quickly with my book friends than my real friends, I noticed, a little sadly.

The doorbell rang. I heard my mother say, "Who is it?" into the intercom.

"Madame Poitier," said the voice. "Miss Pointy."

"Miss Pointy?" My mom couldn't hide her surprise. She buzzed her in. I buried myself under the blanket and closed my eyes. I couldn't stand to see Miss Pointy, not after stealing Luz's sticker, even if she didn't know it was me. And then getting sick! And missing school! It was too embarrassing, too weak. I flopped my arm over the side of the sofa.

"Sahara?" Mom came in. I tried to breathe evenly. Mom clucked her tongue, believing I was asleep. She went to the door.

"Ms. Jones?" I heard Miss Pointy's voice at the door. "Is Sahara here? I brought her homework."

"That was nice of you," said Mom. "Especially since she doesn't do it, does she?"

"Well, it's still hers, to do or not do."

"I guess so," said Mom. "She and Rachel are

sleeping. Won't you come in? Or are you on your way somewhere? Special?" I supposed Mom had just noticed her wardrobe. Miss Pointy must have been wearing one of her party dresses. Or maybe her sparkling tiara. Or her ankle-length leopard-skin coat? I opened one eye, but couldn't see anything.

"I just came from somewhere special," said Miss Pointy.

"I thought you were coming from school."

"I am."

"Oh," said Mom.

"I'm sorry to intrude. I just wanted to drop this off. I know you weren't expecting me. . . ."

"That's fine. I've been home with three sick kids all day, I'm so *bored*." I cringed at the B-word. "Come in for just a few minutes. I have marble cake," said Mom.

I wondered if Mom had her by the arm. The door closed, and I heard the footsteps into the kitchen, the next room over. I heard the kettle bang on the burner. I heard the women sitting together, Mom taking drags on her cigarette.

"Smoke?"

"No, thanks."

"Did you quit?"

"I never quit anything," Miss Pointy said. "I just finish."

"I wish I could finish smoking," said Mom.

"Finish what you start," said Miss Pointy. *Good grief,* I thought, *how do teachers ever have friends outside of school, if they always talk like teachers?* Mom just laughed.

"You're a real teacher, aren't you," she said. "Having any luck with Sahara this year?"

"What do you mean?"

"I mean, considering her history. You read her records, didn't you?"

"No," said Miss Pointy. "I hate reading records. I never do it, until the end of the year. Then it's fun. You can see if other people think you're right or wrong." Mom must have been giving her a strange look, because she kept explaining. "If a kid is wild, or slow, or can't read, it'll show in good time. I have eyes. I don't need those records."

"Seems the records would save time, though."

"Not if they're wrong."

The kettle sang. "So you haven't seen Sahara's file, huh," said Mom.

"Nope. I just see Sahara."

"Well. What do you see?" I knew Mom was holding her breath a little bit. So was I.

"She is going to be a writer," said Miss Pointy. I felt myself blow up suddenly, like a balloon that just had been attached to a helium tank.

"Is she?" Mom finally breathed. "What else?"

"Sorry," said Miss Pointy. "That's all I know about her right now. She doesn't show me a lot."

"Does she write for you?"

"No, not really," said Miss Pointy. "This is good tea."

"Then why do you say she's a writer?"

"I didn't say she was a writer. I said she's going to be a writer. A writer writes. When she starts writing, she'll be a writer," Miss Pointy explained.

"Oh." Mom sounded annoyed. "Well, maybe when she starts practicing rocket science, she'll be a rocket scientist."

"Maybe," agreed Miss Pointy in a muffled voice. It sounded like her mouth was full of cake.

"Except I don't think she's going to be a rocket scientist. I think she's going to be a writer."

"Well, what should I do with this great talent?"

"Read to her. Even though she's a big girl. Leave a lot of pens and paper around the house. Give her a lot of books to read to herself. Probably stuff you've been doing all along."

"You really haven't read the file, have you?" Mom marveled. I thought I heard a little relief in her voice. "You know, she's been held back."

"It'll be great material," said Miss Pointy, her mouth full again. "Great artists suffer. She keeps a journal at school, you know."

"She does?" said Mom. "Can I read it?"

"I lent her the money for the journal. She owes me two bucks," Miss Pointy said abruptly. "Can you advance her?"

"Now?"

"Now's good."

I wondered what Mom's face looked like, fetching the money from her purse.

"Can I read it?" Mom repeated.

"Sorry. Her debt's paid. It's her journal now. You've got to ask her," said Miss Pointy.

"I bought her a notebook too, you know," Mom told her, lowering her voice. "She keeps it in between her mattresses. I sneak to look at it. It's just blank pages and pages ripped out."

Mom!

"*Tsk, tsk.* Maybe she knows you're snooping. Don't be embarrassed. I like snooping, too," Miss Pointy confessed. *Me, too,* I thought. "But either way, she wouldn't rip out blank pages, would she? She's probably writing something on them."

"Like letters," said Mom. I felt a pang.

"Sure. Or stories," said Miss Pointy. "Could be anything, really."

"She does love stories. Reads all the time, here at home," Mom tattled. "She'd rather read than play outside. She'd rather read than go anywhere." *Well, that's not true. Why do you think I read? To go everywhere.* "She's got a great vocabulary, too. She could talk to the queen of England."

"You don't have to sell me, Ms. Jones," said Miss Pointy. "I believe you. That's great."

The women sipped their tea. "Are you going to fail her?" Mom asked finally.

"Oh, I've never failed a child," said Miss Pointy cheerfully. "She, on the other hand, might fail herself."

"Maybe I failed her," Mom said quietly. I bit my lip, hearing Mom's voice tremble. "She's a good girl, she's just a little freaked out. Sometimes she still comes in my room, in the middle of the night. Is that normal, at her age?"

Mom! Do you have to tell her everything?

"I guess, if she's freaked out," said Miss Pointy.

Mom didn't seem to be listening. "Stuck in the apartment all day, you know how it is in the city. Maybe I could have made a better home, worked things out with her father. . . ."

"Excuse me," Miss Pointy broke in. "May I be perfectly honest? You're a class act, Ms. Jones, and you have nothing to feel bad about. I'll put it in your permanent record, if you like. *Good mother. Serves tea and cake without prompting. Just a little freaked out. See Sahara Jones for further details.*"

My mom laughed, but it crackled, like it

might have been a choice between that and crying. "I see why the children like you," said Mom.

"Compliments make me break out in a rash," said Miss Pointy. "Please tell Sahara to get well soon. Rachel, too."

After Miss Pointy left, Mom came in and dropped the homework on the coffee table and went back into the kitchen. I could hear her singing along with the radio.

I tried to go to sleep for real, not because I felt tired, but because I felt sad. Failing other people, I could just say "Sorry," but it hadn't occurred to me that I was failing myself. I didn't want to fail myself. I wouldn't know how to apologize for it. I sat up. Hidden in the pile of homework was my journal. I decided to do the assignment Miss Pointy had given us the day I stole Luz's sticker.

Where I Live
   I live in the city. I wonder what it's like, to live in the suburbs or the country. I imagine if you live in a house, it's easier because you have a yard or a bike and when your mom

sends you on an errand, she doesn't stare out the window till you get back and you don't have to run. I wonder what it's like, not to hear sirens and yelling, not to hear your neighbors. When Mr. Martinez who lives below us comes home from the factory in the middle of the night, he gives himself a wel- come-home party by putting on his Cuban music so loud, his music is full of trumpets and drums and the word corazón, corazón all the time. His music shakes like a bad woman. His music is a bigger woman than his wife, who is small boned, who I imagine is frowning in her housedress because he's sitting on the sofa drinking with his favorite woman. I think this as I watch the crystals on the old light fixture quiver from the throb of his corazón. His coming home is really something.

It's something to me, too. It's someone coming home. I listen for my mother, in the other room. Is she sleeping? Or is she waiting, too? Sometimes I go to her room, but she usually sends me back. She says her bed's too small. She says, Put a pretty picture in your mind's eye, you'll fall asleep, you won't be scared. You don't need me.

So I go back and lie down and listen to Mrs. Rosen, in the apartment above us. Shuffle, shuffle, thump. Shuffle, shuffle, thump. The thump is her cane. I hear her move to the kitchen. The chair scrapes against the linoleum. What is she doing in the kitchen, in the middle of the night? She's nice, she smiles at me on the street, she gave me a butter-scotch candy out of her handbag with the little gold clasp. When she gave it to me, I looked at her hands, wrinkled with more lines than a road map, speckled with lakes of brown. What is it like to be old, I wonder, to have skin with lines for every mile you've walked, for every trip around the sun? When I watch TV, I never want to be old, they laugh at oldness on TV. But in the dark, I hold my hands up straight above me in the air like two stars and I wish for lines that prove I have been here. I wonder about Mrs. Rosen at the kitchen table, looking at the lines in her hands in the middle of the night. Who is she waiting for?

I imagine if you live in the country, you can look out your window and see the Milky Way. Anytime I want I can look out my window and see a thousand other windows, half-shaded or blaring yellow awake. I don't play outside much. I can't swim on concrete. My ears can hardly make out the rattling of the cicadas. But Mrs. Rosen says, life is with people. So maybe I can get along without cicadas.

I looked up and saw Rachel leaning back on her pillow and staring at me. Without blinking, she put out her hand to see what I wrote. I handed it to her, and she read it, her mouth in a line, her eyes moving right, then left. She didn't smile, but when she looked up at me, into my eyes, I knew she saw past the brick, to what is sparkling and moving like Lake Michigan. Good things, exciting things.

10

Orphans

Miss Pointy likes poetry. No, she *loves* poetry. She gives us copies of poems by famous poets, one every couple of days, but she doesn't quiz us about them, so most of the kids throw them in the garbage can about two minutes after she passes them out. Miss Pointy gets mad, but she doesn't make the kids take them out of the garbage can. She says that's our bad choice, all she can do is give them to us, she can't make us take them. Darrell doesn't even look at them, he just crunches them in a ball and pretends the garbage can is a hoop, and uses the poem for a slam dunk or sometimes a three-pointer.

I never throw away the poems she gives to me. I keep them, I memorize some of them. My

favorite is "Autobiographia Literaria" by Frank
O'Hara.

> When I was a child
> I played by myself in a
> corner of the schoolyard
> all alone.
>
> I hated dolls and I
> hated games, animals were
> not friendly and birds
> flew away.
>
> If anyone was looking
> for me I hid behind a
> tree and cried out "I am
> an orphan."
>
> And here I am, the
> center of all beauty!
> writing these poems!
> Imagine!

Frank O'Hara called his poem "Autobiographia Literaria," which means, his life story.
He told it in just a few words, not like me having
to write page after page like this! I whisper these
words I learned from Miss Pointy's inky ditto to

keep myself company when Mom is late coming home from work. The rhythm is sweet, it reminds me of church. *The Lord is my shepherd, I shall not want. When I was a child I played by myself.* I know it is bad to say they feel the same, but I can't help it, it's true. When I'm alone opening a can of corn in the kitchen with dirty dishes piled high, I imagine coming out from behind a tree and being the center of all beauty, which doesn't seem likely, but Frank O'Hara said it happened. All he had to do was come out from behind a tree, and he was Somewhere Else. I say his words over and over again, like a spell, if I say it maybe a thousand times it will come true for me, too. Maybe the poems are a test, like Cinderella's slipper. Maybe if you can make them fit, you can be queen. That would be useful. But not everybody finds poems useful. Not everybody trusts poets, or Miss Pointy.

"Poetry is for punks," said Darrell.

"I'd like to know who isn't a punk, according to you," said Miss Pointy.

Darrell had the answer right away. "People with money."

"Then you should love poets, because they know the value of a word the way a banker knows the value of a dollar. A poem is a small economy of words. Each word is worth its weight in gold."

"Yeah, take a poem to the store, see what it buys you," sneered Darrell.

"If you spend a poem wisely, you'll get love back in return, not breakfast cereal or coffee. We're not talking food stamps here."

Raphael snorted, but it was a clumsy snort, because having a teacher talk about love is so gross you can hardly snort. Still, I wrote out my favorite poem in my best handwriting and I folded it into a little square. I didn't sign it. I tried to think who to give it to.

The door opened. It was Peaches, the Special Needs teacher. I couldn't help slinking down in my seat. She waved to me. I waved back, miserably.

"I'm here for Darrell," she said to Miss Pointy, who was writing on the chalkboard. Darrell started to get up.

"Sit down, Darrell. I didn't say you could leave

your seat," said Miss Pointy. "Where are you taking him?"

Peaches looked surprised. "Services," she said in a lowered voice.

"What services?" said Miss Pointy, not in a lowered voice. "Religious services? I wouldn't have guessed he was Jewish. He doesn't speak *any* Yiddish and his Hebrew is *entirely* illegible. But that's okay. He's a little *slow*," Miss Pointy rasped from behind her hand.

Peaches laughed. I recognized that laugh, an oh-I-heard-about-*you* laugh. "We don't like the word *slow*," said Peaches.

"We don't?" said Miss Pointy. "Then what do we do about snails and turtles and broken watches?"

Peaches straightened. "Miss Poitier, Darrell Sikes need special help. He has been *identified* as having *impulse control issues*," she said, even lower than before. "He acts out."

"Who doesn't?" Miss Pointy asked.

"No, I mean . . . haven't you checked the records?"

"Oh, wait! The records! The *records*! Oh, yes!

Darrell Sikes! You'll have to excuse me, I'm new! Ha-ha! Now let me see! I got a note about his *serv-ices* . . . just recently . . . there has been a change, now where did I put that note? Oh, I am so disor-ganized! Didn't you get a copy? The first week of school? About the change in Darrell's *services*? Hmmm. . . ."

Watching her, I realized I had a front-row seat to some serious and amazing lying. She wasn't looking for anything at all, she was just touching everything on her desk. First she lifted the flower vase, and then she opened a drawer; then she ran her hand over some files, and then she started rifling through a pile of papers. Then she made clicking sounds with her tongue and opened another drawer and swished her hand on the inside so you could hear all the scissors and paper clips and stapler removers clattering around. "Oh, where *is* it!"

I told myself not to jump to conclusions, but even Darrell Sikes was making a constipation face to keep from smiling. Why, why, *why*? Why would a teacher want Darrell Sikes in class, let alone *lie* to keep Darrell Sikes in class? Especially after all the trouble his psycho mother had stirred up. Especially after George Washington and his cherry tree. What happened to honesty and accountability? Why would she lie to help a crazy bad boy like Darrell Sikes? *Darrell Sikes!* It was a mystery to me.

Finally, Miss Pointy turned to Peaches and said, very decisively, "*You* must have it."

"Me! I don't remember getting any note," said Peaches. "What did it say?"

"It said, Darrell's mother has refused services this year. No pullout."

Peaches touched her lip. "You're kidding." The she lifted her arm and pointed straight at Darrell, who was pretending to be very interested in the wall. "The note said *he* is not going to be receiving services? H*im*?" She looked kind of excited, like she had been told she had won the lottery but she still couldn't quite believe it.

"Isn't it a shame?" Miss Pointy made her eyes wide. "You can call his mother. Maybe she'd be willing to talk." She smiled innocently. "Or go to the principal and tell him you lost the note. But I'm *sure* that's what the note said."

"I guess we could try it." Peaches looked worried. "I hope, though, you will come to me if you need, you know, *support*."

"That's very kind," said Miss Pointy. "I'm grateful for the offer."

Peaches brightened. "And Sahara?"

"Yes?"

"How is she . . . doing?"

"Gee, I don't know," said Miss Pointy. "Sahara! How are you doing?"

"Fine," I said in a small voice.

"Good," said Miss Pointy. "She's just fine, thanks for asking. And how is . . . your mother?"

"Fine," said Peaches. "Fine."

"Oh, that's excellent. Everybody seems to be fine."

"All right," said Peaches. "Then I'll be going."

"Fine," said Miss Pointy. "Thank you! Bye now!" She walked Peaches to the door.

Miss Pointy sat down at her desk, which she hardly ever does, and smiled behind her fingers.

She and Darrell were staring at each other. "She's a nice lady," said Miss Pointy.

"Yes, she is," said Darrell sternly. "And yet you behaved very badly."

"Uugghh," she grunted, holding her stomach. "I think I have impulse control issues." They both burst out laughing. I don't think I had ever heard Darrell laugh before. Oh, it was nice, rattling and light like a tambourine at church!

I dropped "Autobiographia Literaria" on Darrell's chair as we were heading out to recess.

"Sahara, may I see you?" Miss Pointy caught me at the classroom door. "Please stay behind. I need to speak with you for just a minute."

Speak to me about what?

She left me alone in the room while she walked the rest of the class to the exit.

I saw the pile of journals on her desk. I had been doing the journal assignments every day since I had been sick. That couldn't be it. Luz's journal was on top, stickers sparkling. I swallowed hard. I couldn't even think about if she knew how bad I was.

Did she see me drop the poem on Darrell's desk? I didn't mean anything big by it. Sometimes people just need a poem sometimes, didn't she say so? Was she going to talk to me about boys, in which case I would truly have to die? Maybe she knew I was snooping in Darrell's journal. Just once in a while, and just *Darrell's*, it's easy to find in the pile because it's all beat up and anyway you can hardly read it, the spelling is so bad. I don't even know why I would read it, it's just he is kind of surprising, it's not like he'll just come out and talk to you like a regular old boy. She said she liked snooping herself, didn't she? But I can't tell her I know that, because I was kind of snooping *then*, too, by pretending I was asleep and listening.

But what if it wasn't about Darrell at all?

Oh well, here it comes, I thought. "*Wouldn't life be easier if . . . ?*" She'll talk to me like I'm *special*. Maybe I'll have to sit out in the hall again. Maybe she read my file. Maybe . . .

Miss Pointy swept back in. "Sorry," she said.

"Miss Pointy, sometimes I look in Darrell's journal!" I exploded.

She froze for a second, and gave me a funny look. Then she unfroze. "Well, don't get caught," she said. She went right for the pile of journals, but Luz's journal was flung to the side, and so was Darrell's. She dug sloppily until she pulled out my own journal, with my name written in my tight little handwriting on the cover.

"This." She held it in the air and shook it like a lawyer on TV. "This."

I stood in front of Miss Pointy, but she didn't say anything more for a moment, just stood there shaking my journal. "Y . . . yes?" I squeaked.

"You'll excuse me, but I need to ask some things about *this.*" Miss Pointy glared suspiciously down her pointy nose. "You're not involved in any *time-travel* debacle, are you? Like, you didn't go a few years into the future, write this, and *come back?*" She leaned forward and squinted at me in an accusing way.

"N . . . no, ma'am," I said. "I don't think so."

She took out a pair of glasses from her desk. X-ray specs, with spirals covering the lenses. "Hold still," she demanded. "Nothing personal.

Just doing my job." I nodded as though I understood. She stared into my face, hard, I think as hard as anyone has ever looked at me besides my own mother. I couldn't see her eyes, but her eyebrows were going up and down like she was trying to crack a safe or defuse a bomb. "*Extraordinary!*" she whispered. "*It's all there!*"

"What is?" I asked.

"Words," she said. "Your *talent.*" Then she pulled something out of her tight sleeve. A gold star, with a rainbow streaming behind it, just like the one I had taken from Luz. "Well, that's all I needed to know," she said. "Run along."

I burst onto the playground. Rachel and Cordelia were waiting for me. "What did Miss Pointy do to you?" asked Cordelia, but I ignored her and rushed past, across the playground. To Paris.

"What?" asked Paris. I took her hand and slipped the sticker inside, secret-like. She looked at her palm, and then at me. She didn't smile, and she narrowed her eyes. But she closed her hand around it, nodded and ran off. To Luz.

I felt myself breathe again.

I could hear feet clumsily drumming toward me as Cordelia and Rachel raced to catch up. "You in trouble?" huffed Rachel.

"No," I said. "Not anymore."

But I was wrong. When we came back in the classroom, I thought Darrell would sit on the poem I left for him and that would be that, but he saw it even though I folded it so small. He opened it, and opened it, and opened it, he didn't even sit down. Then he read it, and then his face turned a purplish color and he looked mad. He looked so mad I got scared and slunk down low in my chair.

He yelled a swear word that I know I shouldn't write, and the whole class looked at him. Then he roared, "Who put this on my chair!" as deep and loud as an angry giant. I thought about climbing into my desk, but I figured I wouldn't fit. "I ain't no orphan!" He nearly screamed. "Somebody's calling me an orphan!"

"Nobody's calling you an orphan." Miss Pointy was looking so exactly the other way of me that I knew she was thinking about me. How does she know everything? I hoped Darrell wouldn't notice. His chest heaved up and down and he looked at all of us with red, wet eyes.

I could have cried from feeling scared, and I could have cried for being so terrible, for nearly making the meanest, most special boy in school explode.

But all I could think of was how it would be at least a week before I had the chance to snoop in his journal again. And how Miss Pointy was right. Poetry is not for punks.

11

Why Teachers Get Apples

$\mathcal{I}$t had rained, and the fallen leaves made the sidewalk look like the floor of the kindergarten, spattered with red and yellow and green paint. Miss Pointy was telling us another story. It was about a teacher. We listened as we pressed leaves into our leaf identification books. Miss Pointy wore a crown of red maple leaves that she had stapled to some construction paper. It looked pretty against her green hair.

"She was very old."

"How old?"

"Old enough for gray hair. Old enough for a small hump in her back. Old enough for a squint in her eye." Miss Pointy squinted. "She walked to school. She got up early in the morning, so early in the morning that the dew was still on the grass."

Raphael burst out laughing. "Did she step in the *dew*?"

Miss Pointy's eyes slid, warning him. "As a matter of fact, she did, since the dew was droplets of water, *Raphael*. As she walked, the toes of her shoes grew wet from the *dew* and made little wet half-moons at the tips of her shoes.

"She lived out in the country, and every day she took the same route, down the brown path through the woods, across the clearing, past the play yard and to the school."

"Why didn't she drive her car?"

"It was before cars."

"My grandma's old, and she drives a car. A Buick LeSabre."

A few kids called out the makes of cars their grandmas drove. "I can wait," said Miss Pointy. And she did. "Anyway, if you ever lived in the country, you'd know why she didn't drive her car. She wanted to see the part of the day when the sun and the moon are both in the sky at the same time, on opposite ends."

"I seen that," nodded Angelina knowingly. "Uh-huh. That pretty."

"I like it, too. It reminds me of two children at opposite ends of the playground, two girls who haven't met, who are too shy to come together." I looked at Rachel and smiled. She smiled back. I felt Paris looking at me and turned around. "In the country, the air smells like snapped green beans, and the crickets are playing their legs. *Be-deep! Be-deep!*" sang Miss Pointy.

"And every time you take a step, a mess of them jump out of nowhere, uh-huh!" Angelina was getting excited. "That how it was at my grandma's house this summer. Miss Pointy telling it true."

Miss Pointy looked at Angelina while she spoke. "And isn't there something about being alone when you walk in the country, early in the morning, listening to the leaves as they whisper and twist like a hundred thousand tongues of silver-green, straining to tell a secret only to you?" We all looked up from our projects, expecting her to turn into a tree from the way her voice went soft, like a breeze. "A tree has its own language. If you knew how to listen, a tree could tell you a story for every ring in its trunk. A story about the storm whose lightning struck it in the spot where children used to climb, or about the bad-tempered squirrel who decorated its drey with diamonds that fell out of a burglar's sack, or about how the tree mourns for the old owl who was so swift and quiet, he could catch shooting stars in his claws."

"Maybe the tree was just trying to say 'Good morning,'" said Luz.

"Maybe," agreed Miss Pointy.

"Or nothing at all," said Rachel.

"Or nothing at all," repeated Miss Pointy. "Or maybe just humming. Or going over tree times tables." We groaned.

"Maybe tattling," said Janine. "Do trees tattle?"

"I expect so. Most everyone tattles at least once."

"Sakiah more than once!" Dominique called out. Everyone laughed.

"Miss Pointy! Dominique is making fun of me!" Sakiah whined.

"This is stupid. Trees don't talk or tattle or

none of that baby imagination stuff. Trees is just trees," Darrell reminded us.

"That's the spirit, Darrell. And teachers are just teachers. So this one teacher walked to school every day, past the trees, magical like Angelina's trees. . . ."

"Uh-huh!" nodded Angelina.

"Or not magical, like Darrell's trees, we really don't know," Miss Pointy confessed. "But the teacher sometimes thought they might be magic, because sometimes their knots looked like eyes and mouths and their branches looked like noses and arms, but that also could have been more baby imagination." Darrell looked smug. "She walked past these trees, into the clearing where she saw the big black crows sewing their bodies through the sky. Then, as she walked along further, she saw the farmer's horse cantering along the edge of the clearing."

I scratched *cantering* lightly onto the cover of my notebook.

"Finally she saw the schoolyard full of children."

"Sounds like a nice walk," said Janine.

Miss Pointy wrote the word *idyllic* on the board. "It was so nice and gentle and full of country charm, it was *idyllic*. But after twenty-five years of this walk, she started to get a little jealous of the things she *encountered*, or came across." I wrote these words down, too.

"What you mean, 'jealous'?"

"She would see the birds and think, 'Why can't I fly?' She would see the horse and think, 'Why can't I run?' She would see the children and think, 'Why can't I play?'"

"That's goofy," Larry remarked.

"To make matters worse, there was a boy in her class—"

"Was his name Raphael?" asked Raphael.

"Was it Dominique?" asked Dominique.

"Was it Ernie?" asked, guess who, Ernie.

"Oh, no, I can't remember his name," said Miss Pointy, with her mint-in-the-mouth smile. "I just remember he was a bad boy."

"Was his name Darrell?" asked Veronica. We laughed.

"Shut up! If he bad, that mean his teacher bad," snarled Darrell.

"You're right, Darrell!" Miss Pointy pounced. "You're exactly right! This boy was bad, but he was the same bad as his teacher, for different reasons. At home, he was beaten. He was poor. When he walked to school, the trees didn't talk to him. When he came to school, the children didn't talk to him. After some time, he started feeling jealous, too. 'Why can't I read? Why can't I write? Why can't I have friends?'" We became quiet.

"He couldn't act angry at his father, or he would beat him," Paris suggested.

"He couldn't act angry at his classmates, or they'd beat him," Kiarre added confidently, like she'd be first in line.

"So, who was left? Every day, he'd be angry at his teacher. It was old times. She could have beaten him. Those were the days!" Miss Pointy sighed. "But in twenty-five years, she hadn't beaten a child. She didn't want to beat him."

"She had to love him," said Rashonda. "Teachers are paid to love children."

"Teachers aren't paid much, so they don't love us much," said Larry. Miss Pointy stared at Larry, surprised. "Most don't love us much," he corrected himself.

"That's silly, Larry. Teachers aren't paid to love children. You can't legally pay someone to love you," Miss Pointy explained. "Loving children is what teachers do for extra credit. It's not the main assignment."

"Seems to me that the extra credit is more important than the main assignment," observed Cordelia.

"You're right, smart Cordelia," said Miss Pointy, taking out the Happy Box. Cordelia looked surprised, and took a long time to choose a star. "Extra credit is done of your own free will. Work and love given out of free will is always more joyous, better-quality stuff."

Raphael gagged. "Quit talking about love! Get back to the boy who got beat."

"Okay. So there's this boy and this teacher, neither of them working for extra credit. The boy being as mad and mean as he can to the teacher. Puts a tack in her seat, chalk in her eraser."

"Old-fashion mess," grumbled Darrell.

"And the worst part is, he talks back. Talks back like crazy. He won't do a thing the teacher says. He stands up on his desk and beats his chest and shouts."

"Like King Kong!" breathed Ernie.

Darrell stood on his chair and demonstrated.

"Thank you, Darrell. Like that. Well. The teacher doesn't know what to do. Every morning she walks to school, she thinks so hard about this bad boy, she doesn't see the moon or the sun or hear the trees talking. Her mind is so full of the hard day ahead."

"Girlfriend needs the trouble basket," observed Kiarre.

"Uh-huh." Janine and Kiarre slapped hands.

"She sees the birds and the horse and the children, and her heart starts to crack. Things that made her happy as a younger person were the very things that made her sad as the days wore on.

"Every day, the boy wouldn't do his work.

Every day she felt the lashes of the boy's words, like a whip against all her years of service."

"She should beat his ass!" Rashonda exploded.

"School language," reminded Miss Pointy. "Rashonda, do you think that would really work?"

"Nah. But she'd feel better."

"Yeah! Make her beat his ass in the story!" urged Raphael, also forgetting school language.

"Yeah, he beating *her*, you said so! 'Words like a whip!'"

"Make her whip him back!"

"Let's vote! Who says, 'Whip his ass?'"

"We are not voting," said Miss Pointy, her arms crossed like she does when she's waiting. "Stories are not a democracy. Thank God." Finally, we quieted down.

"I'm disappointed in you," she said finally. "She didn't beat him. I told you. She hadn't beaten anyone in twenty-five years, and she wasn't going to give this boy the satisfaction of breaking her record."

"You go, girl!" whispered Kiarre.

"One day, she gave the children an

assignment. 'What I wish.' They had to write in their journals."

"They had journals back then?"

"She was ahead of her time. After she gave the assignment, she realized she gave it because she wished someone would give it to her." *Like when I ask Rachel a question*, I thought. "The teacher took out a blank piece of paper. The teacher wrote simply, 'I wish I were a bird. I wish I were a horse. I wish I were a child.'"

"Three wishes. She greedy," said Leon.

"She should of wished that boy out of her school," grunted Tanaeja.

"Well, at that very same time, the boy wrote his wish down. He wrote, simply, 'I wish she was not a teacher at this school.'"

"Why he write that? He could have written anything. He could have wished for a million dollars."

"He wrote that because he knew his teacher would read it. He knew it would hurt her. He wanted to hurt somebody, because it felt like somebody was always hurting him.

"That afternoon, at the end of the day, the teacher collected the papers, took her bag of books and left the school, walking back past the schoolyard, the clearing, and into the woods.

"The next day, when the boy came to school, his teacher wasn't there. There was a substitute. He felt a little scared."

"What for?" asked Cordelia. "It was just a wish."

"Then he felt so sorry and wished her back and they lived happily ever after, and all the trees sang and danced, tra-la," said Darrell.

"If you think you've got a better ending than I have . . ." Miss Pointy said, sighing.

"Be quiet, Darrell," warned Dominique.

"The replacement was mean. He beat the children, he beat the boy, too, first time he opened his mouth. This new teacher would have none of that. The children didn't defend the boy, they were tired of the way he acted in class and were glad he was being controlled. The new teacher saw the boy couldn't do much, and he didn't call on him. It was nice at first, but then the boy started to feel invisible and empty. He worried that it was his wish that made this happen. But he had nobody to ask about it, no one to assure him that his fears were silly.

"One morning he was walking along the path, and he heard something that he had never heard before. It seemed to him that the trees were talking, in a language he had heard all his life yet never had come to understand. He stood still, between the school and home. Frightened, he ran off the path, and when he stopped running, he saw an apple tree. This cheered him up, and he forgot his fear. He pulled some fruit from the tree, and ate on the way to school, the hungry knot in his stomach unwinding slowly.

"When he arrived at school he was so satisfied that he skewered his last apple on the fence post.

"Out the window, he could see the apple being visited through the day by a little bird. He watched as the bird flew in wide circles, around and around the school, alighting now and then on the apple to eat and sing. The boy felt another knot unwind within him.

"Time passed. Every day, he picked apples

from the tree and stuck one on the post for the bird. One day, he decided to see if there were any other trees in the woods. That's when he found his old teacher's bag, sprawled on the ground, and under his teacher's damp books was the last assignment he had done for her. Reminded of his terrible wish, he wondered if wishing it had made it so. But he only wondered for a moment, because he was older."

"Had more sense," said Larry.

"Did he? Well, he took the books and dried them out. Every day after school, he studied them on his own."

"Why'd he do *that*?" Raphael laughed.

"It beat going home," said Darrell. I looked at him, maybe everybody did. Miss Pointy, too.

"Now a horse started visiting the post where the boy put his apple. He'd gnaw it off in a bite or two, and then gallop around the clearing. Can you imagine how nice it was for the boy, watching that beautiful, free creature?

"More time passed. Do you know what happens when time passes?"

"People get old," said Sakiah.

"People die," said Rachel.

"Both those things happened. The boy got older. His father died, and the mean teacher retired and moved away. So the superintendent came in, the boss of the schools. He drilled the class with review problems. The boy who had been so bad shone like a star. The superintendent asked if he would like to teach at the little school when he graduated that spring. He said yes.

"When the leaves began to fall," Miss Pointy said, picking up some dried leaves from her desk and letting them somersault on to the floor, "the doors of the schoolhouse were open, and behind the desk sat a young man with the start of a beard and a mind full of knowledge. No one could have guessed that he was once a hungry little boy who stood on his chair and thumped his chest and was beaten with a strap by his father, no one could have guessed that he had wished his teacher away, or that for all that evilness and sadness, he still remembered to stab an apple on the post every day for his bird and his horse.

"He stood at the door and rang the bell, and the children who were playing in the yard came running to the door and filed inside. In came a little girl with brown hair pulled tight, and freckles and sunburn and a smile so wide you would think her pigtails were stretching her face."

"The third wish!" gasped Angelina.

Miss Pointy smiled. "The little girl had in her hand a big red apple. She handed it to the man.

"'What's this for?' he asked the girl.

"'This is for all the days when I was a bird, and all the days I was a horse. You gave me an apple every day, and now I will give an apple to you.'" Miss Pointy took the apple off of her own desk and put it on Darrell's desk. Darrell just watched her face, and pretended not to notice the apple.

"Every day the little girl gave her teacher an apple, paying back the small favors of his boyhood. The other children saw this and thought she was trying to be the favorite, and they started giving the teacher apples, too. But in his heart, the little girl who had once been his teacher was indeed his favorite. And as the days wore on, there was no little girl happier to be a little girl and no grown-up happier to be a grown-up than the two at that school, and their satisfaction was such that there was never a need for another wish. The end."

"What kind of story is that?" asked Darrell.

"I made it up," said Miss Pointy. "From a dream I had. You like it?"

"It's not a real story if you just made it up, is it?" wondered Leon.

Yes, it is, I thought. *It will be real as soon as I write it down. It will be a real story about a girl who wished it were real.*

"I like it," said Sakiah.

"You would," said Darrell.

"It's a fairy tale," said Angelina.

"Ain't no fairies, or royalty," said Veronica.

"It's a *pourquoi* tale," said Paris. We had learned that *pourquoi* means "why" in French, and *pourquoi* tales explain why things happen. "It tells why teachers get apples."

"Maybe you're both right," said Miss Pointy.

"Maybe they're both wrong," said Sakiah. "Sounds to me like a fable."

"A fable's got to have a moral at the end," Ernie reminded her. Sakiah wrinkled her nose and stuck out her tongue.

"So if this is a fable, what's the moral? The lesson?" asked Miss Pointy.

We were quiet, thinking, and watching other kids think.

"What goes around comes around," blurted Larry.

"Tit for tat," snorted Raphael. Dominique snorted, too.

Miss Pointy ignored them. "Hmmm, I don't know, Larry. Try to put the moral into your own words, not a cliché, something people have said before."

We thought some more. "Wishes come true," said Luz.

"Good try," said Miss Pointy, "but I don't know if that's a lesson that is always so. What else can we come up with?"

"Wishes are powerful," said Dominique.

"Good," said Miss Pointy.

"Things change. They don't always stay the

same," said Cordelia. "Like, you don't have to stay a kid."

"That's a good one, too. Anyone else?"

"School is a powerful place where things change and wishes come true," Paris said slowly. "It's a place where you can grow up, if you let yourself." It sounded like a kiss-up answer. It also sounded right.

Miss Pointy took out her Happy Box. We all looked on jealously as Paris chose a sticker. "Anyone else?" We all looked at each other. Paris's answer seemed good enough; it got the Happy Box, didn't it? "What's the lesson?" Miss Pointy insisted. We were all quiet. My wrist twitched, and I started to raise my hand.

The bell rang.

"Oh-oh," said Miss Pointy. "Put away your leaf books and let's go."

"You spent all that time telling us a story," accused Cordelia.

"Do you want me to apologize?" asked Miss Pointy. "Fine. I'm sorry we didn't have time for our journals today. Write in them tonight, if you like.

What *you* would wish for." We stood up and gathered our things. I imagined what everyone would write:

> I want a castle of stickers with a special sticker room, no, a hundred rooms all filled with stickers and a real unicorn that I could ride . . .

> I wish I was invisible so I could walk home without anybody bothering me . . .

> I wish I didn't have to watch the baby after school, I never get to go out . . .

> I wish for a robot that looks just like me who would take my tests . . .

> I wish I was a superstar in the WNBA . . .

My file, I thought.

I wish for the letters in my file.

Miss Pointy yelled over the scraping and clonking sound of us turning chairs upside down, putting them on our desks, and the noise seemed to wake me up from my daydream. That's a silly wish, I thought. Of all the wishes! Wish for a million dollars. Wish to look in Miss Pointy's closet and get to choose any dress I want. Wish Daddy would come home. Wish for something silly like that. . . .

Quick, I wrote a P with a line through it over what I had scribbled.

Miss Pointy stood at the door and said goodbye to each of us. Rachel stayed behind and started making her watery stripes across the board with the sponge.

Miss Pointy grabbed me by my jacket hood. I hung behind. "I saw your hand. So what do you think that story was about?"

"Paris said it."

"Really?" Miss Pointy leaned against the

threshold and crossed her arms. "Stories mean different things to different people."

Should I tell her? I looked at the floor. She waited. I waited, too, but I *wanted* to tell her. "People thought that boy was one way, but . . . inside each person, I think there's a secret person," I said.

"Huh," she said. "That's interesting. Do you have a secret person inside of you?"

"No . . ."

"Yes she does," announced Rachel, from across the room, not looking up from her chore.

"Yes," I corrected myself. I could not look at Miss Pointy. "But only you know my secret. You and Rachel." Rachel kept on wiping the board, but she had that same mint-in-the-mouth expression that Miss Pointy wears.

And there was Miss Pointy, wearing it too. "I don't know if that's true," she said. "Secret people are hard to keep inside. Especially if they are wonderful. You, for instance, are leaking." I looked up, feeling shy. She was smiling, but her eyes were serious.

When I left the room, the hall was empty, but Paris and Luz were leaning against some lockers. They looked up when they saw me. They cast long shadows in the afternoon light that came through the exit. *They're going to beat me up,* I thought. *They're skinny, but there's two of them. If they're wearing rings, I'm done for.* I walked and could hear my footsteps clicking.

"Hi," I said as bravely as I could.

"Hi," said Paris. She looked nervously at Luz, who looked nervously back at her and stuck her thumbs in the straps of her backpack. *Well, this is a very polite way to start a fight,* I thought. *Oh, my God. I'm going to get beat up by the nicest girls in school.*

"We were wondering," Paris said. "We're thinking of starting a club."

Oh?

"For people who like books," she went on.

"And esteekers," added Luz. "Do you like esteekers?"

I looked at Paris, who pursed her lips. "I guess," I said.

"And I know you like books. So we were wondering if you'd like to be in it," said Paris.

"Who else is in it?"

"Just us," said Luz.

"For now," said Paris, then added quickly, "but anyone who wants to join can, though, right Luz? We don't like to leave people out." Luz seemed to both nod her head yes and shake her head no at the same time, in total agreement. It was contagious. I shook like a bobble-head.

"When's the first meeting?" I asked.

"I don't know," said Paris. "Let's talk about it while we walk home. We go your way. Can you be at the library this Saturday?"

"Sure," I said. "You know what? My mom works at a restaurant, and after the meeting we can go there and eat all the pancakes we want for free."

"Wow!" they said.

Yeah, wow! I thought, as we walked out the door together.

My wish by Darrell Sikes

Ok ok I am a orfin! I wish for a friend.

    a. You are not an orphan, you live with your mother and

    b. You already have a friend.

    a. your not supos to look wen I write p at the top and

    b. dont gimme that teecher mess

    a. Sometimes I snoop and

    b. I'm not your friend, I'm your ally.

    a. My moms not my frend shes my mom and

    b. I dont have anthin to write for letter b

    a. You've got a friend in this

classroom right now and you
don't even know it. Why don't
you keep your eyes peeled?

b. I also don't have anything to
write for letter b.

c. Wait, I just thought of a b. See
me, I need to help you with your
punctuation.

How is it Im posed to keep my eyes
peeled
     No id never be able to peel my eyes
and look for a frend oh no no no cant be
helped so wood you mine peeling my eyes
for me sins you are kine enugh to show
consern in that ragard

     HAHA

12

Name-calling

"*I* think I've told you enough stories to choke a horse," Miss Pointy said, surprising us the next afternoon. "I'm in the mood to do some listening. Remember I suggested a while back that you could write stories in your journal about how you got your name? I was thinking that maybe some of you wouldn't mind reading those aloud."

This was very exciting, because, of course, we were not allowed to read other people's journals without their permission (even though I had snuck again and read Darrell's the other afternoon). Miss Pointy passed them out. Several kids waved their hands in the air. "Pick me!" "Pick me!" In my imagination, I raised my hand, but then in my imagination, she called on me and I had to read it, and kids yawned and threw paper at me. So

instead of raising my hand, I slunk down in my seat and smiled at my classmates. I was eager to hear what they had written.

"Ernie? You have your hand raised so quietly." Boys who weren't called on groaned. "Come, stand in front of my desk so we all can hear you."

"My full name is Ernest Meija the Second," he read, "and I was named after Ernest Meija the First, my mother's brother. He is a fireman with the Chicago Fire Department. He was the first child born in this country from my family. He helps my family a lot. He has never been killed on the job, but he had a friend who was. He told me when he is fighting fires he always tries to save the family pet if he can. I think he is very brave and I am proud to be named after my brave uncle Ernie."

He looked up, finished.

"Comments?" asked Miss Pointy.

"Your uncle Ernie sounds cute," said Mariah.

"Yeah," agreed Janine and Cordelia.

"How old is your uncle Ernie, Ernie?" asked Miss Pointy.

"He's around thirty, I think."

"Too old for you, girls," said Miss Pointy. "And hundreds of years too young for me."

"How old *are* you?" asked Sakiah.

"In human years, or teacher years?" Miss Pointy answered, and then quickly called on someone else.

"That's nice, he saves cats," said Larry.

"Ees good," said Boris, who hardly ever talks. He was smiling openly at Ernie, his friend. He looked like a proud poppa. Ernie blushed.

Miss Pointy looked pleased. "Well done, Ernie!" Some thin applause. "Who else here has been named after a family member?" Many hands went up. "It's nice to have a family name with some history. Paris? Your name has some history, too. Why don't you step right up."

Paris cleared her throat.

"'My Name,' by Paris McCray. My mother and father named me after the capital of France, the city of love and romance. For instance, in France they love pancakes called *crêpes*. I know how to make them, my mom showed me. They love poodles so much that they let them eat in the restaurants like people. There is an Eiffel Tower there, and many great churches, and many artists went to live there, including but not limited to the great Josephine Baker, who danced naked before it was in style to do so."

"Woo!" said Raphael. "I see London, I see France!"

"It is all very exotic," Paris continued, "and furthermore people speak French all the time, for example. I do not know how to speak French, but I hope to learn in high school. My mom and dad never went to France. They were going to go, but then my mom got pregnant. It was a surprise because my parents already had four kids. They needed the money more than the trip, so my mom said if we can't go to Paris, then Paris will come to us. Someday I will go to Paris and wave from the top of the Eiffel Tower to my parents who will be eating crêpes down below. The end."

"That was good," said Veronica.

Cordelia disagreed, and showed it by gagging. "Naked people! Dogs in restaurants! Paris sounds like a filth hole!"

"Oh, Cordelia, be quiet," said Tanaeja. "You don't even know what you're talking about."

Cordelia jutted out her chin. "Excuse me! I have been to France, and speak fluent French!"

This was, of course, the wrong thing to say in front of someone named Poitier. "*Est-ce que c'est vrai? As-tu mangé un croque-monsieur quand tu as visité? Moi, j'adore les croques-monsieurs, presque plus que les crêpes.*"

"I'm sorry." Cordelia sniffed. "I'm afraid I only speak *northern* French."

"*Naturellement,*" Miss Pointy said innocently. "I was merely wondering how you found the grilled cheeses over there."

"I found them extremely filthy," said Cordelia.

"Really! I found them delicious. I also found your paragraph delicious, Paris. Very romantic. *Vive la France!*" We applauded especially loudly, just to spite Cordelia.

"*Vive la* Paris McCrepe!" cheered Dominique. Paris bowed elegantly.

"I wish I had me a plane ticket to France," said Kiarre.

"Would you like to go, too, Kiarre?" asked Miss Pointy.

"No. I'd just love to send Cordelia and get her lying self out of this classroom."

We laughed. "Now, now," said Miss Pointy, "kind words in the classroom." She didn't say Cordelia wasn't a liar. And Kiarre said sorry, but she said it more to Miss Pointy than to Cordelia. I felt a little sorry for Cordelia. Just a little.

"Paris wasn't the only one who was named after a place. Sahara? Would you read what you wrote?"

Me? I hadn't been up in front of a class in at least a year. Or two years. Didn't she know that about me? Suddenly, I wished she were the kind of teacher who looked at records.

"Sahara?"

There it was again, she was calling my name. I tried to feel my legs. They felt like two Popsicle sticks with all the Popsicle melted off. I shook my head, no.

"Oh, come on, Sahara," said Miss Pointy.

"Please?" coaxed Paris.

I looked at Rachel. She smiled, and nodded her head, excited.

"I'll go, then," Cordelia sighed, like she was being inconvenienced. "'Cordelia Carbuncle: Ruby of the Seven Seas.'"

"Sahara, just get up and read your damn thing!" Kiarre barked. I teetered forward.

I stared down at my journal entry. I felt all eyes on me, I felt the room tilt just slightly. "I didn't check the spelling," I confessed.

Miss Pointy shrugged. "Neither here nor there."

"It's personal," I whispered hoarsely.

"All good writing is personal," she whispered hoarsely back. "Pretend you're reading somebody else's writing, you'll get through it."

"It's weird," I pleaded. "It's long."

"Not as weird and long as waiting for you to do this," said Miss Pointy, not whispering. Embarrassed, I turned to face the class. "Take a deep breath," she suggested, behind me. I did.

"'My Name,' by Sahara Jones," I began.

"Louder," she ordered.

"'My Name,' by Sahara Jones," I said again.

"Louder, and with expression!"

I swallowed. "'MY NAAAAME,' by SaHAra JONES!" I yelled. The class laughed.

"Good," said Miss Pointy. "Go on."

I can see how my daddy thought my name was a good idea at the time I was born. He must have thought that naming me after the biggest part of Africa would make me special. But special wears off. At least, it did for my daddy. He left me and my mom when I was in the third grade. We're not sure where he is.

When he left, Mom changed our last name back to Jones, which was her name before she got married. "You can change your first name, too, if you want," she told me. "We don't need nothing that man gave us."

That last line wasn't so hard to write. Why was it so hard to read? I swallowed again.

"Go on," said Miss Pointy. "You're doing great."

I didn't mind my name, and I didn't exactly agree with my mom, but I didn't let on. It's not every day that

your mother gives you permission to change your name.
"Okay," I said. "Call me Shaquana."

"Shaquana!" My mom wrinkled her nose.

I heard the class laugh. It startled me. I found my place again and kept reading.

"Jennifer?"

"Girl, I know you're joking," Mom said. "Put a little more thought into it than that. A name's got to last a long time."

I ran through lots of names in my mind for a few days. Aisha. Candace. Saundra. Camille. Shalonda. Dolores. Denise. It made my head spin.

One day we had a substitute, and during science she showed us a video about the great African desert, the Sahara. A few kids laughed and pointed out that I was named after a desert, but once that was said, nobody seemed very interested in the video. Except for me. I was finally going to see what my father named me after.

The sand had ripples all through it, like it was remembering water. A sun dipped down at the edge of the horizon. It shook in the waves of heat like a great orange fist. The desert beneath spread flat and dry, knowing that under its sands lived scorpions that are especially venomous, snakes that can smell the taste of you, tortoises that know no time. The desert is mystery. To cross it, you have to be a camel. You have to use what you have for yourself, keep what you need inside your-self, in a big sagging hump. A camel only spares enough to spit. This is the way to survive the desert, I thought, as they showed the darkness of night leaning over the dunes.

As the video played I could hear the winds picking up as the desert night grew colder and colder. I felt my own teeth chatter, and I couldn't stop them. I wasn't Sahara, the girl, anymore. I was Sahara, the desert, filled with secret scorpions. And even though I know that deserts are very dry places, I started to cry and cry and cry.

I guess somebody told the teacher, because the next thing I knew, she was kneeling next to my desk saying, "What's the matter, honey?"

And I told her, "I think I'm having a heart attack."

She looked back at me like maybe she was going to

have one, too. She made me open my mouth and say "Ahhh," like you can tell if someone is having a heart attack by looking down her throat. She pulled me out of my seat and dragged me down the hall to the office. But as soon as I was out of that classroom and away from that movie, I felt better right away.

"My name is Sahara," I said to my mom, first thing when I came through the door. "Sahara Jones."

She looked at me in such a way, I wondered if she was swallowing a pill.

Finally, she said, "Wish I'd-a thought of it first."

But my name has changed since my daddy left. I didn't change it, and neither did my mom. Last year when I was in Special Needs, some kids started calling me Sahara Special. I know they were saying it to be mean, but now I like it anyway. My names are given to me, but they are also names that I choose to take. And the choosing makes all the difference.

"I stopped writing there because the bell started ringing. Plus, I was finished anyway," I said. There was silence. "So, the end." There was still silence.

My leg was shaking so hard, I felt like I wanted to hold on to it with both hands. My palms were sweating, and my heart was pounding. I could not bring myself to lift my eyes from my journal. There was no noise. Were they still in the room? Were they all asleep? Were they still *alive*?

"Comments?" said Miss Pointy.

Still nothing. Out of the corner of my eye, I saw Darrell give me a funny look.

"Come on," urged Miss Pointy. "Let's give her some feedback."

"Well, what you want us to say?" Angelina finally said.

"Actually, I have some notes here," Cordelia cleared her throat. "I think she meant to say, 'I was finally going to see that after which I was named,' not 'I was finally going to see what I was named after.'"

Michael's voice even rolled its eyes. "What's the difference?"

"The difference is English," said Cordelia.

"She speaks English. There's plenty big words,"

said Janine. "How'd she know all those words like
. . . what'd you say?"

"Darkness of night leaning over the duuuuu-
unnnnessss," hummed Angelina. "Tortoisessssss that
know no tiiiiimmmmmmme."

"Yeah, like that! How'd she know all those
words like that!"

"Yeah, she writes like a grown-up!" said
Raphael. "All that 'he said, she said.'"

"I read a lot," I mumbled. See, they hated it!
They thought it was weird! They thought I was
weird! I *was* weird! I blinked; I would not cry in
front of them.

"Maybe she copied it from somewhere," said
Leon.

"No, she didn't," came Rachel's voice. I was surprised to hear it. "She told me this summer that
she was going to be a writer, and she is going to
write a book."

"A real book? In the library?" Ernie was
impressed.

"Uh-huh," I said. Luz leaned over and whispered something to Paris, and they both looked at

me, excited. I bet they were planning the next meeting of our club, for people who like reading *and* writing. And . . . uh . . . esteekers.

"What's it going to be about?" asked Sakiah.

"No, no, no!" Miss Pointy stood up. "Don't ask writers what they're writing about. If it comes out of their mouths, it won't come out of their pens."

"At first, I thought it was funny. Then it wasn't funny at all," said Ameer.

"It was *great!*" yelled Paris. I looked up.

"You got a good imagination," said Rashonda.

"Girl-I-di-int-know-that-you-could-write-like-that!" rapped Tanaeja. "Sahara-how-your-journal-get-down-like-that!"

The class laughed. I would have laughed, too, if I hadn't been so terrified.

"Sorry I said you copied," Leon said. "I just . . . it was good, Sahara."

"Yeah, Sahara," said Sakiah. "*Wow.*"

"I theenk Sahara should get an esteeker," said Luz.

"She did," said Miss Pointy. "It's on her journal."

"I thought it was long," said Raphael. Everyone

ignored him, except for Tanaeja. "Course you did," she cooed, and patted his hand. He snarled at her and pulled his hand away.

"Well, what's the point of Sahara's story?" Everyone settled down and looked at one another. "Ernie? You're good at morals. What do you think the moral of the story is?" Ernie shook his head. "Anyone?"

"Don't judge book by its cover," came a voice.

"Who said that?" Miss Pointy looked around. "*Darrell!* I'm so proud of you!" She grinned so that all her teeth showed, and Darrell smiled back the same way, mimicking her.

"Yay, Darrell!" said Raphael.

"Don't make a stink about it," said Darrell.

"Yay, Sahara Special, then!" said Mariah.

"Yeah, yay, Sahara!" said Tanaeja and Kiarre.

I looked red-faced to Rachel, who was nodding and back to her quiet self . . . but this time I didn't mind, not one bit.

The whole class cheered. They cheered so loudly, I couldn't hear my heart breaking. But I could feel it. I guess Miss Pointy could see it. "And for such inspirational writing, Sahara can be messenger and deliver this note for me. And Cordelia, you waited so patiently. It's your turn."

The class groaned, more jealous about my messenger job than they were about my writing. "As I was saying," Cordelia started up. "'Cordelia Carbuncle: Ruby of the Seven Seas.'"

I took the envelope and stepped quickly out in the hall. I wiped my eyes on my sleeve and leaned against the wall. Then I looked down at the envelope, expecting to see OFFICE, or a room number. It said SAHARA.

I opened it.

The note said, *Turn left.* So I turned left.

The note said, *Walk three paces.* So I took three steps.

The note said, *Turn left again.* So I did, and I was facing an old locker.

We weren't allowed to keep things in lockers because the upper-grade kids kept stealing lunches from them. So the lockers were used as storage for old textbooks. The note said, *Open.* So I opened the locker.

There was a small cactus in a pot, with a beautiful red flower in bloom at the top.

And behind it, a brown folder with my name on it.

My file.

The classroom door opened. Out stepped Darrell, holding the boys' pass. He closed the door, and faced me straight on, head bent, eyebrows bent, frowning.

"What?" I squirmed.

"You sent me that dumb poem, didn't you." I was too embarrassed to deny it. "I am *not* an orphan," he said.

"I know." I squirmed some more.

"And," he said, "neither are you."

He walked away, whistling, toward the boys' room. I reached behind the cactus and pulled out my file. I clutched it to my chest with both arms.

13

Autobiographia Literaria

I ran into my room at home and closed the door. I couldn't wait.

I spilled the envelope out on to my bed. On the top was a page ripped out of my journal that I had forgotten about.

Do teachers have secrets?

Yes. For instance, I like to give kids presents sometimes on the sly if I know what they really want. That's a good secret. Teachers' bad secrets, like getting caught smoking in the custodian's office or being fresh to the principal or having boyfriends that ride motorcycles, are kept in a dreadful file *somewhere. It's hard to get to a teacher's file. But student files are so easy to get your hands on.*

Next in the pile was a letter from my mom. "I request my daughter be removed from the special education program." I smiled and turned the letter over.

And then, there were the letters I had written.

Dear Daddy, I miss you. . . .

Dear Daddy, When are you coming home. . . .

Dear Daddy, Why didn't you take me with you. . . .

Dear Daddy, It was my birthday, I wished it on my candles that you would call, and you didn't. . . .

Dear Daddy, Mom says you don't help with anything anymore but I don't care, I know you'll come back and help us. . . .

Dear Daddy, There's a hole in my heart. . . .

I turned them over, one by one, like cards in a fortune-teller's deck. But these weren't telling me the future, these were telling me the past. It was sad to see them, but it was funny, too, that they had kept them. Even though as I leafed through them I realized they all said the same thing, they all told the same story.

Miss Pointy says, the main character is the one who changes.

I held one of the letters I had written in third grade up to the light from the window. I couldn't help smiling at my round, careful cursive. *Dear Daddy, Can't you see from my handwriting what kind of girl I am, will that make it enough for you to come home to me?*

The clouds outside were high and generous big, moving fast. I opened the window. I closed my eyes and held out the piece of paper, let it flutter in my open palms. When I opened my eyes, I saw it flapping in the sky like a bird, flying away.

I tossed out the next letter, and the next, making birds, until the last one. As I watched them tumble past the brown brick of the buildings, east,

east to the lake, I wrote one last letter in my mind's eye.

> Dear Daddy,
> I love you. I miss you. I hope someday you're smart enough to be sorry, but if you're not, that's okay. I'm smart enough not to keep all this in my file.
> Love, your daughter and secret writer,
> Sahara Jones, now and forever

In my mind's eye, I ripped it in half. In my mind's eye, I let the pieces loose, let them climb the stairway of the wind past the buildings, past the lake, past the moon and stars and sun, to Somewhere Else, the place where my father now lives.

And then, I pulled out my notebook and wrote, and wrote, and wrote. Not about my *Heart-Wrenching Life Story*, but all these pages about a teacher and her *Amazing Adventures* with her class, all about a teacher's file and a teacher's secrets. I wrote about friends and tattletales, bravery and fear, but for the first time, it didn't all have to be straight true, I could write about all the exciting things I wished were true. The words moved like wheels across the paper. I didn't count pages or minutes. Mom tapped on my door, and only then did I notice the sun had gone down and I was writing nearly in the dark. The whole apartment was warm. The radiators clanged like music. I could smell meat loaf in the oven. Mom had fried potatoes with lots of onions and butter. She was making my favorite meal for dinner. Where had I been?

"You've been sitting in here forever." My mother flicked on the light switch and squinted at me. Had I? It was like magic, like Rip Van Winkle, who fell asleep and found himself a hundred years older when he opened his eyes. I unfurled my fingers, fossilized and aching around the pen.

"Dinner's on."

"Almost finished."

"Whatcha writing now?" she asked.

"Sketching out some adventures," I confessed. "I've already finished my *Autobiographia Literaria*." In

one second I was embarrassed that I was so eager.
Mom's eyes were laughing at me.

"Who, now?"

"My life story. I have had a very interesting
life," I said, defending myself.

"Me, too." Her eyes were glinting. "Fascinating.
And it's over?"

I ignored her. "I'm starting something new."

"Maybe you'll show it to me sometime?"

"If you want," I said. "It'll be in the library." I
felt her bristle. Did she think I was being fresh? I
turned in my chair to correct myself, to explain
that it *was* promised to the library, behind section
940, to be found by someone in the future, someone whose life will be made more exciting just by
reading my *Heart-Wrenching Life Story and Amazing
Adventures.* But the doorway was already empty.

While we ate, I could hear the silverware
against the plates.

"It's good, Mom," I complimented her and
smiled. She smiled back. She looked at me for a
long time. It made me nervous, so I looked at my
meat loaf.

"So, what did you do at school?"

I shrugged. "Kids read aloud from their journals."

"Lord, they sure waste your time at school, don't they?" said Mom. "Just writing and talking about any old thing that pops into your head. Bet them kids in the suburbs learning calculus by now." She didn't know what to say next, I could tell. "You're growing up," is what she finally came out with.

"How do you know?" I teased.

"You're not talking to me." She smiled sadly.

"I talk to you," I filled my mouth with potatoes.

"I guess I don't know how to speak your language."

I laughed a little, like she had made a joke, like we were talking about why firemen wear red suspenders or what time it is when an elephant sits on a fence, and she laughed, too. We ate the rest of the meal in thoughtful silence.

But that night, I climbed into bed with her, and she didn't say anything against it. She held me firm with one arm around my shoulder, like she didn't want me to go anywhere. I stared at the ceiling and felt uneasy and excited at once, like I was destined to end up Somewhere Else anyway, no matter how she held me.

"Sing to me," she said, half-joking. "Tell me a story. Tell me your autobiographia whatever."

I took a breath. I thought about what poem to spend. I spoke to her softly, like I was singing a lullaby.

```
When I was a child
I played by myself in a
corner of the schoolyard
all alone.

I hated dolls and I
hated games, animals were
not friendly and birds
flew away.

If anyone was looking
for me I hid behind a
tree and cried out "I am
an orphan."

And here I am, the
```

```
center of all beauty!
writing these poems!
Imagine!
```

Imagine, I thought.

She gently stroked my hair, making sure I was there. It was comforting, but now, I didn't need it. It was extra credit.

ESMÉ RAJI CODELL

is an avid collector of sparkly stickers and a pretty good roller skater. She is also the author of *Educating Esmé: Diary of a Teacher's First Year*, which won an Alex Award, given for the best adult books for young adults. She has worked as a children's bookseller, teacher, and school librarian, and now runs the popular children's literature Web site www.planetesme.com. Esmé lives in Chicago with her husband and son.